Rule's Obsession

LYNDA CHANCE

Print Edition

Copyright © 2014 by Lynda Chance

All rights reserved. This book or any portion thereof may not be reproduced or used in any manner whatsoever without the express written permission of the author or publisher except for the use of brief quotations in critical articles or reviews.

This is a work of fiction. Names, places, businesses, characters and incidents are either the product of the author's imagination or are used in a fictitious manner. Any resemblance to actual persons living or dead, actual events or locales is purely coincidental.

ISBN: 1499150555
ISBN 13: 9781499150551

Dedication

For Clayton and his rules, the only reason my life isn't total chaos.

Angie followed Damian's secretary across what seemed like miles of plush carpet and walked into the office when indicated. She was still in a state of shock; she'd found out in the reception area that he didn't merely work in the downtown high-rise, he owned the building.

She heard the door snap closed behind her, and with her heart catching, she faltered just inside the large room. Her gaze was caught and held by dark eyes as Damian leaned against a desk of solid mahogany while standing completely still, obviously awaiting her arrival. His eyes were both sharp and hooded, his body held in a pose of relaxation that seemed inconsistent with the almost tangible electricity that radiated from him in waves.

Her pulse pounding, her footsteps stalled completely. Before she could get a word out, he pushed off the desk and began to track her across the office, his muscles corded and his eyes reflecting a sheen of purpose. The space between them narrowed rapidly as his eyes fell to her throat and then scanned her body quickly before lifting to her face again.

Any semblance of a smile dissolved as his expression hardened imperceptibly; a raw sizzle filled the air as his brooding features reflected a harsh, atavistic hunger that almost brought Angie to her knees as he stood not six inches away in all his tall, masculine glory.

He stood almost indolently for the beat of three seconds before reaching out and seizing her with a dominant force that gave her not an ounce of choice in the matter. He mumbled two words, "Thank fuck," in a guttural rasp that, had she realized it, contained an evocative foreshadowing of his future intent where she was concerned.

Rule's Obsession

Chapter One

Damian Rule sat in the reception area of the sports-themed hair salon and wondered for the hundredth time why in the hell he continued to come to this place. It was inconvenient, far out of the way of both his condo and his downtown office. Furthermore, the ambiance was intrusive; the lighting was harsh and a continual stream of commentaries about sporting events that he didn't give a shit about blared from several flat-screen televisions scattered around.

As he surveyed the room with set features, he acknowledged that the employees who worked here and the clientele that frequented this establishment weren't the type of people he usually mixed with. But he'd come in one day out of desperation for a haircut when he'd been on this side of town, and he'd been coming back ever since. True, the stylist here did a fairly decent job, but certainly not so amazing that he couldn't do without her.

As the woman in question came to get him for his appointment and immediately started babbling and rummaging through the top drawer in her unit before she began, Damian tuned her out and let his eyes wander around the part of the room that he could observe from the reflection in the mirror.

He didn't see what he was looking for right away, but he continued to watch the mirror. The place was busy; it always was. Several stylists moved around, either standing at their stations tending to cuts, or leading customers to and from the row of sinks. After a few more minutes of patient observation, his diligence was rewarded with a slight motion at the back of the store that caught his attention. Ahhhh...*there she was.*

Her dark head was bent over something she was mixing in a small bowl, and at the sight of her feminine form and downcast eyes, Damian felt the same tightening in his groin that he felt every time he saw her. As he continued to watch her, he acknowledged to himself exactly what it was that kept bringing him back to this particular salon time and time again. He didn't come here for the location, or for the stylist who cut his hair, or for the sporting events that were broadcast during business hours. It was none of those things.

It was the woman he was looking at now. The stylist who held his attention, the one who went by the name of Angie.

Damian rolled the syllables through his head and let the connotation of the name bring an image to his brain. Angie. Angela. *Angel.*

His mouth twisted into a smirk. Angel. *Yeah, right.*

The girl didn't resemble an angel in any way, shape or form. Unless, of course, you counted the fact that she could undoubtedly take him to heaven with those full lips of hers.

Fuck.

He needed to get her out of his mind; he knew he did. But how the hell was he supposed to accomplish that when he kept letting his dick lead him back here every time he needed a damn haircut? He'd been coming here, watching her *for months.* It was absolutely, undeniably, *fucking amazing* that Damian had been able to sit still and only observe her for this long. She did shit to his insides, that...*fuck*. He took a deep breath and steeled his guts. He didn't want to think about what she did to his insides.

Unable to fight the compulsion, he continued to watch her, as if his eyes were magnets drawn to metal. His cock swelled against his jeans as he studied her. Yeah, an angel, she wasn't. In fact, she was possibly just the opposite. Although she moved with an unconscious grace, the girl certainly wasn't peaches and cream; no, she had the darkly intoxicating look of wickedness about her. She was a feminine, appealing, *begging to be fucked* little devil.

She was a hot, slender, gothic mess.

She looked to be about medium in height, maybe smaller, but he couldn't really tell because she always wore black platform heels that boosted her height and made the legs beneath the black fishnet stockings look amazing. He had no way of knowing if she always wore short skirts, or if it was just his luck, but every time he saw her, she was in a skirt so short it almost made him come, just from watching her. She was totally amazing, totally fuckable...absolutely fuckable enough to keep him coming back here just to get another look at her, over and over again, no matter how much he fought against it.

Each time he walked in here, he expected to find that his mind and his libido had only been playing tricks on him. There was *no way* she could be as hot as he'd imagined the time before.

But she always was.

She was always hot, but she wasn't always perfect. Sometimes she looked weary, indisputably tired. But when her make-up wasn't impeccable and her smile wasn't firmly in place, those were the times when he wanted to fuck her the most, when she looked almost vulnerable, and he wanted nothing more than to pick her up and wrap her legs around his waist and plow deep inside.

He shouldn't like to see her weary, but he did, because when she was noticeably tired, those were the only times when she'd slip up and actually let herself take a peek at him. Most of the time, she blatantly ignored him.

Dressed as she was, it would seem as if she'd have an attitude, but she didn't. It was incongruent with the way she looked, but she didn't put out vibes, she didn't try to flirt with him, as most women did.

She ignored him as if he didn't exist. It made the hunter inside sit up and take notice, but he always tamped it down and remained in control. But when she was tired and he caught her looking at him from beneath her long eyelashes, his insides would combust with heat and his veins would fuel with lust. His imagination would run rampant and he'd imagine himself stomping across the room and hauling her off her feet, sinking his hands into the soft flesh of her ass and carrying her to the room in the back. He'd strip her until she was butt-assed-naked and then he'd fuck her standing up, he'd come hard inside of her and she'd melt around him, her core hot and wet while she exploded in ecstasy around him.

The fantasy of fucking her screwed with him every time he came in here, and it continued to screw with him every time he left. In his brain, he'd already fucked her every way possible and then some. He'd fucked her standing up, he'd fucked her on all fours, he'd fucked her in his office while restraining her to his desk.

He gritted his teeth and swallowed hard, trying to dispel the image, but he couldn't. He'd had bad, *bad* thoughts about this girl. Never, ever before in his fucking life had he had thoughts like he'd had about her.

Usually when he thought about fucking, it was *only* about fucking. It was about relief. But not with this girl. He wanted to restrain her. *He wanted control.*

He took a deep breath to steady his nerves and let his gaze run up and down her length, almost against his will. He tried to focus on the reality of the situation and attempted to push the fantasies from his brain. But the reality kept intruding; he wanted to fuck her more every time he saw her. And his analytical brain knew the reason why. It was because she was *so* wrong for him.

She was exactly the opposite of the kind of woman he usually went for. The exact opposite of the kind of woman he needed to eventually marry. One who would take her place by his side and give his home life the type of conservative grounding that he needed, staying in the background while he expanded the family business. Whether he liked to or not, he was forced to entertain on numerous occasions, and those times would only increase the larger and more varied the Rule Corporation became.

He knew what he needed; he needed someone perfectly coiffed, someone who dressed conservatively, someone highly educated who could entertain his guests when the time came. But not the woman his mother had been hinting at lately. Never her. He at least needed to be attracted to the woman he'd eventually marry, and Courtney Powell didn't even make his cock twitch, no matter how sweetly pretty she was. She was nice enough, pleasant even. But he'd known her since she was a small child, and the close relationship their respective mothers had shared had left him with an almost familial feeling toward her.

Although the woman his mother kept pushing at him would never do, he realized that he did need someone from his world, not someone like the gothic witch across the room who wore spiked cuffs on her wrists, chains that hung from her belt, and a skirt so short her ass almost showed. He needed someone polished, not someone who wore black eye shadow and purple lipstick. He needed someone refined, not someone who looked as if she chanted to the dark lord of the underworld and wanted nothing more from him than to drink his blood.

No, the girl he couldn't drag his eyes away from was none of the things he needed in his future, so she might as well be off-limits to him. He ran his hooded gaze up and down her body again in almost painful regret. He needed a wife and she was so fucking unsuitable.

But so perfect for the fucking he wanted to give her.

Angie turned away from delivering the color she had mixed for Rita and practically slammed into a clearly panicked Janice. The woman's face was pale and she held her cell phone clutched to her chest. "I've got to go. *Like right now.*"

A sliver of immediate concern landed in Angie's stomach. "What's wrong?"

"The school called. Bethany's running a high fever and throwing up."

"Oh, poor baby. Okay, no problem; I've got you covered."

"I'll run go get her and then I'll call and cancel my last two appointments from home, but can you take care of him?" Janice's eyes grew even wider as she tipped her head in the direction of the man who Angie had begun thinking of as *Damian, the Devil Incarnate.*

Her heart skipped a beat as she focused on him. Her stomach tripped up with butterflies, but she pasted a look of bravado on her face that she was far from feeling, so that her friend would be reassured. "Sure. I'll take care of him. You go on. Take care of Bethany."

"Thanks. I've already washed his hair. I'm going to grab my stuff and hit the road, okay?"

"Yep, no problem," Angie answered as she reached out and gave Janice a quick hug, feeling the tension in the other woman's frame. "Are you sure you're okay?"

Janice shook her head and Angie was shocked to see tears in her friend's eyes. The other girl looked back at Angie as if making a huge confession. "I'm sinking financially. My credit cards are so close to maxed that it's not funny. When Danny walked out on us, he took everything and left my credit in shambles. Just coming up with the co-pay for the doctor is stressing me so much that I feel sick."

"Do you have enough?" Angie asked with concern.

Her friend blew out a breath. "Just barely."

"What about the prescriptions? Do you need some help with those?" she asked.

"No, I think I've got it covered."

Angie felt a shot of anger at the absentee father. Danny had been a dick galore and that wasn't anything new. But Janice had hidden her financial problems so well that Angie hadn't had a single clue. "Try not to worry, okay? Focus on getting Bethany well and then we'll think of something. I've got some savings, I can help you out."

"I can't take your money, Angie."

"We'll see. I know we can think of something. At the very least I'm damn good at squeezing a dime out of a nickel." The two women hugged again, and after they parted, Angie went to the back room and slowly counted to ten as she took a few stabilizing breaths before going back out to face what she knew she must. Looking at herself in the mirror, she inhaled deeply and tried to calm her shaking hands before turning toward the door with determination.

Damian looked passed his reflection in the mirror and watched, entranced, as *Goth girl* walked up behind him and immediately began babbling, "So Janice had to leave because her kiddo is sick. I'm Angie and I'm going to cut your hair today if that's okay?"

Her voice was feminine and husky, and his brain temporarily short-circuited as all the blood in his body seemed to pool to his groin at the mere thought of her even touching his hair. He gritted his teeth, fisted his hands around the arms of the seat to keep from grabbing her and locking her to him. *Could he sit still while she touched him without reaching out and picking her up and carrying her out of here?* He tightened his abs and nodded once in answer to her question and watched in fascination as she lifted a black comb to his scalp.

Her hands looked delicate and soft, with beautiful slender fingers that ended in tapered fingernails. *Fingernails painted black.* His insides clenched with arousal, but his brain fought the involuntary reaction to the inappropriate sight.

Her black-tipped fingers were trembling subtly and without thinking about his actions, he lifted a hand and wrapped it around a blue-veined wrist. "You okay?" he bit out.

She raised her eyes to his in the mirror, licked her lips and sucked in a deep breath. He could see the pulse beating visibly in her throat but she didn't answer him. He'd bet his last dollar she *couldn't* answer him, and he knew in that second that he affected her the same way that she affected him.

Well, shit.

Good fucking luck trying to stay away from her now, Rule.

The guy was hot, no question about it. And he was even hotter up close like this. But *Jesus,* that didn't mean she had *to tremble,* did it? She glanced at him in the mirror and was able to clear her throat and get her vocal chords working enough to answer his question. "Yeah, I'm fine. You just want a trim, right?" At her words, his grip tightened on her wrist, sending a heated rush to the juncture of her thighs, but then he dropped his hand back to the arm of the chair.

"Just a trim." His voice was low and brusque, and Angie felt the deep cadence reverberate down her body in a current of sensation.

Unable to stop the movement, she ran her fingers through his hair, as if to gauge the length. As she slowly started the cut, she studied him. Probably early thirties, he always wore a bespoke suit and he kept his hair severely short. He was conservative, no mistaking that. She'd bet he absolutely *hated* the fact that he was attracted to her. And it was obvious that he was. She'd caught him watching her more times than she could count.

But she didn't care to be noticed by a guy like this; he seemed just like her father. Angie knew that deep down, she loved her dad, but she admitted they didn't have a close relationship, even though he'd been a decent enough father. He'd taught her more about money and finances than she could ever possibly need to know and he'd made sure she could stand on her own two feet before he'd moved across the country. But her father had an addiction that she didn't care for. *Women.* Her mother had died when she was young and since then, Angie had known more stepmothers than she cared to think about, because her father became bored very easily.

And *Damian the Devil* had that same look about him. Was she judging him, probably unfairly? Yeah, she was, but she didn't care.

Janice had told her weeks ago that he had asked about the way she dressed and there had been disapproval in his tone. He didn't care for her clothes. And that suited Angie perfectly. And it was true that she didn't care what anyone thought of her; she damn sure never wanted to be noticed by a control freak like she was sure this guy was. She didn't care how freaking good-looking he was, she didn't care how fast he made her heart race, it didn't matter how quickly she thought she could drown in his bedroom eyes if she wasn't careful.

Did he look like he knew what to do in bed? Absolutely. But Angie had no time for a guy like this one. No time and no desire to be tempted. So it didn't bother her that too-conservative men like him usually stared a little too long before looking away. Being left alone by businessmen of his ilk was a fringe benefit of the gothic style she'd created for herself.

It wasn't as if she was truly gothic; she admitted she was just a poser. She'd started dressing in black because she'd found a couple of adorable outfits at the mall, and the reaction of her male customers at the salon had been more than positive. Her tips had almost tripled every time she'd worn black. She was a fairly quick study, and after the unexpected influx of cash, she'd taken on the persona with relish, buying tons of accessories and developing a heavy hand with her make-up. Dyeing her hair black had given her pause, but it didn't have to be permanent, and she knew any damage caused by the chemicals would eventually grow out.

Now, as Angie cut his hair, she didn't try to make conversation with him, and she refused to look at him in the mirror again after finding his eyes glued once to her face, and then frowningly, to her breasts. Her tiny, barely-there breasts, hidden beneath a flimsy bra and her favorite tight, black *Nine Inch Nails* t-shirt.

His brows were furrowed as he studied her shirt, and the harsh look on his features sent shivers of heat through her system. After intercepting that look, she avoided meeting his eyes again. Instead, she concentrated on giving him the perfect cut, and she soon became lost in the feel of his damp hair beneath her fingers. When had giving a haircut ever seemed so intimate? It was insane really, because she gave cuts all day long, mostly to men and boys, who were the type of clientele the salon attracted. So why did she now have to become aware of exactly how close she stood to this particular man, what his hair felt like sliding between her fingers, and the way his eyes stayed fastened to her as if he wanted to strip her naked?

She was lost in uncomfortable thought when his deep voice intruded. "You're very pretty," he announced in a low, gravelly tone that sounded as if the words were ripped from his vocal chords against his will.

The words sent a libidinous heat down her spine that she tried to ignore. She found his eyes in the mirror and quickly looked away before answering curtly, "Thanks."

Without looking at him directly, she noticed that his attention became even more scrutinizing. "How old are you?"

Unable to help herself, her eyes landed on his in the mirror again. "How old are you?" she fired back, without answering his question.

"Thirty-four." His lips flattened. "And you?" he demanded, his dark brown eyes holding hers hostage.

"Twenty-seven," she managed shortly, wishing he'd mind his own business.

Silence permeated the air between them after her answer, and it was all Angie could do to keep her hands from shaking.

Finally, the cut was finished and she handed him a mirror to inspect her work. He took it and held it up with a grunt of semi-approval. She pulled the protective covering from his shoulders and shook it out as he stood to his feet.

With little to no fanfare, he pulled a bill from his wallet. As she stared down at the large denomination note, attempting to get her frazzled brain to function, he murmured, "Keep it," and turned and strode out the door.

A couple of weeks later, Damian stood mixing a drink at the sideboard in his mother's living room when her statement finally penetrated his brain.

"You want me to do what?" he asked in a booming voice, freezing in place.

His mother set her coffee cup down and nervously stood up and shut the door so they couldn't be overheard. She made her way over to him before quietly answering, "I want you to consider pushing forward with your relationship with Courtney, and I think that my dinner party on Saturday night would be a good time to start."

Damian closed his eyes for a moment in pure frustration before opening them again and looking straight at her with determination. "You have got to be kidding me. There is *no* relationship between us and furthermore, you're very aware of that fact." How in the hell could she think that he felt anything but a familial type of love for Courtney? When his mother had brought the girl home after the death of her parents, Damian had already been out on his own and she'd become almost like a second little sister to him. He hated to admit it, but he'd mostly ignored her, slotting her in with Erin, the youngest of his siblings, and now when he thought of them, they were almost one unit, 'the girls.'

"She's a perfect girl, Damian. You've been playing the field for far too long and you owe it to your father's memory and the company that he left to you and your brothers—"

Damian gritted his teeth and cut her off. He loved his mother but she'd gone too far this time. "Mother, I need you to listen to what I'm about to say, okay? I don't want to hurt you, but you need to start understanding how it is. *How it was.*"

His mother stared at him with a sheen of tears in her eyes. "Okay."

"I love you; I loved Dad. You know that." He cleared his throat. This was damn hard for him, he did love his mother and he and his siblings had always tried to protect her from pain of any kind. At her nod, he continued, "I know you love Courtney like a daughter and she's a sweet girl, but I don't feel the way you want me to feel about her and you've got to quit trying to control me through guilt." He watched for a sign that she was registering his words. "Even if the company had been in the black and worth millions, you shouldn't keep reminding me of the fact." His eyes narrowed. "But Mother, the company was in the red, in a big way, and you know that it was. The only thing that Nick and Garrett and I inherited was a truckload of debt. There were *no* assets. Zero freakin' assets, Mother. The company was on the verge of bankruptcy. You have no clue how much easier it would have been if we'd just walked away from it all." He studied his mother, who was listening to him in silence. "But we didn't do that. We honored our father's debts, we kept you in the same house you'd been living in since you married him, we put Erin and Courtney through college without a quibble and if we've done anything wrong, it was protecting you and the girls too much from the real world."

He took a deep breath and watched closely to see if she would accept the truth this time. It was a fact that his mother lived in her own little fairytale world, and if there were two truths he knew about her, the first was that she loved her children more than anything else, and the second was that she always had her head in the clouds.

She reached up and touched his cheek gently, the gesture full of so much love and tenderness that he almost groaned. *How was he supposed to stick to his guns when she was the kindest, most compassionate person he knew?* She watched him a little sadly. "I know, sweetheart, I couldn't have survived without you boys and I'm so sorry there weren't more liquid assets when your father died." But then she tilted her head and looked at him as if *he* was the one who didn't quite understand. "But there was that life insurance policy, and the company itself was still intact and doing business. You boys inherited the business, and just look where it's at now." She smiled and patted his hand as if the world and everything in it was perfect.

Damian shut his eyes for a moment in temporary defeat. The life insurance she spoke of had only been enough to pay off the loans that had been called in the day after his father's death. It hadn't put a dent in the rest of the debt. They'd barely had enough to pay for the funeral, and the amount of business debt that had been left after the insurance had dried up had been staggering to him and his brothers. It would have been so much easier for them to walk away from it all, to start a new business from scratch. But they'd manned up, and together had decided to take on the debt and to rebuild the family business from the ground up.

But his mother would *never* understand. She continued to believe that they'd been left a fortune, and she probably would until the day she died. *And it was their fault.* They'd worked their asses off, and in the beginning, put everything they had into making sure their mother and the girls never had any hardships.

It was time to try a new approach with her. If telling her that he wasn't interested in Courtney in a romantic way wasn't enough to convince her, then he'd have to bring out the big guns and prove it to her another way.

He'd have to show her.

Putting a long and stressful day behind her, Angie walked out of the salon and made her way across the parking lot toward her car. There was one thing she craved more than anything: a hot bubble bath. Her muscles were sore and her feet were screaming at her to *sit*.

Digging her keys from her purse, she hooked the strap across her chest and was almost to her car when she glanced back up. Her steps immediately faltered as she recognized the tall man lounging against a vehicle parked next to hers, directly next to her driver's side door. Over six feet of muscle-packed male leaned against the gleaming black Mercedes as if he owned the world and everything in it.

She recognized him immediately, of course. The air became lodged in her throat at the same moment she realized butterflies were going crazy in her stomach.

When she refused to come any closer, *the Devil Incarnate* stood to his full height and raised an arrogant eyebrow as he challenged her, *"Now what are you going to do?"*

Biting the inside of her cheek, Angie crossed her arms over her chest defensively. "What do you mean by that?"

"Look around you, sweetheart. It's pitch-black and there's no one around. What if I were a stranger who meant you harm?" His eyes blazed, shooting arrows of flame. "What the fuck would you do? Those ridiculous little razor-blade earrings wouldn't help you."

Angie took a moment to calm her racing heartbeat as she studied him. It *was* evening, but it was far from pitch-black; the parking lot was well lit and although his purpose for being here was dubious, she didn't think he meant her any bodily harm. "Maybe I have a gun," she dared him caustically.

He lifted his eyes heavenward as if she didn't have a working brain cell in her head and then glared at her again. *"Do you have a gun?"*

Of course she didn't have a gun. "Are you a stranger who means to do me harm?" She shot back, repeating his words to him, wanting only to get to the bottom of why he was accosting her like this.

"If I were, honey, you'd be in the trunk of my car by now."

Chapter Two

Angie saw his hand swing out as he indicated the sleek black vehicle he'd been leaning against.

She let out a controlled breath and tightened her arms over her chest. "What do you want, exactly?"

For mere seconds, the look he gave her was raw; it held a sexual sizzle that produced a masculine scowl and then his features went blank and his eyes became hooded. "You screwed up my hair."

And he waited so long to complain about it? She stood up straighter and took immediate offense. "I damn sure didn't."

"You always cuss for no reason?" he questioned hotly, as if grilling her were his supreme right.

"Only when I *fucking* feel like it," she slammed back, trying to piss him off but not really sure of the reason why.

His nostrils flared and his gaze dropped to her breasts and then to the vee between her legs. The moment began to feel surreal to Angie as he watched her as if he wanted to find the closest horizontal surface and shove her down onto it. All she could do was try to control the trembling in her legs and moderate the oxygen she pushed in and out of her lungs. After an abbreviated silence, he asked, "You always wear black?"

Angie sucked in a breath at the blatantly sexual look on his face and retaliated quickly, "You always hit up on women you barely know?"

"Only when I want to fuck them, and I'm *not hitting up on you*," he answered succinctly, animosity dripping from his voice.

Her eyes flared at the intended insult and then she narrowed her gaze on him. "You're crude. Get away from my car and go the fuck away."

He seemed to ignore the observation about his character and went back to the subject of the cut she'd given him. "Look what you did to my hair." He turned until his profile was in her direct line of vision.

She couldn't see anything wrong with his hair from where she stood. It was damn perfect, just like the rest of him. He had broad shoulders sitting atop a lean body, a chiseled face with a bone structure so masculine that she had to swallow before she could form an answer. "What's wrong with it?"

"You screwed it up. It looks like shit."

"That's bullshit. Is that your lame excuse for coming here to see me?"

He raised a single eyebrow. "What if it was?"

"I'd say you're stalking me then."

He studied her as if trying to delve inside her thoughts. "That's not the reason I'm here. But you do need to fix my hair."

"Whatever."

"I'm serious, sweetheart."

"I'm not your sweetheart. Don't call me sweet—"

He spit out a laugh that contained no humor. *"Who the hell would want you for a sweetheart?* I'm sure nobody could ever trust you enough to fall asleep around you. You'd probably drive a stake through their damn heart."

Angie couldn't decide if he was just plain rude or over-the-top, obnoxiously rude. She could definitely see a gleam of sexual heat in his eyes, no matter what he said. She opted for the response that wouldn't give him an opening into what she figured he really wanted from her. *"Fuck you."*

A deadly stillness came over his form and his mouth flattened while his eyes lit up. "Bring it on, baby."

A wave of heat rolled down her spine, but she immediately ignored it. If this was a come-on, it was one unlike any she'd ever come up against. "In your dreams, Mister. Go away."

"I'm not going anywhere until you agree to fix my goddamn hair."

She sighed in resignation. "Okay, fine. Come in on Friday and I'll fix it."

"I need it fixed by tomorrow morning."

"Well, that's a problem because I don't work again until Friday."

"You can fix it tonight. Right now. We can go back to my condo."

Her stomach clenched tightly and her fragile control almost snapped but she held it together. "You've got to be kidding me. After you just threatened me?"

He took immediate exception to that and stood to his full height, the aura of casualness leaving his stance. "How the hell did I threaten you?"

"What was all that bullshit about strangers and harm and it being dark outside?"

"They weren't threats for God's sake, it was concern," the words were ripped impatiently from his throat.

"Concern?"

He raised a single, arrogant eyebrow. "You think you're bulletproof, darling? Has it occurred to you that you might attract unwanted attention in that get-up?"

He glanced away and looked around the parking lot before leveling his gaze on her once again. Who was this guy who thought he could give his opinion on how she lived her life? She tried to temper her response. "We're in a safe neighborhood. Nothing's going to happen."

He shook his head with a pained expression but changed the subject. "I need to talk to you."

Finally. Now they were getting somewhere. She knew this wasn't about his damn hair. "About?"

"I don't want to discuss it here. You want to go somewhere else?"

She'd give him a minute of her time because he'd been coming to the salon for a long time, but go somewhere with him? "Um, not really."

"Look, I don't mean you any harm, but I need a favor."

Okay, now that sounded a bit too intriguing to ignore, even for Angie. "A favor?"

"Yeah," he answered curtly.

Angie studied him a moment, trying to take his measure. When she answered him, she opted for a touch of humor. "Something to do with the fact that I give an outstanding haircut?"

A look hardened his features. "No. Something to do with the fact that even though you're wearing skull-themed bling and purple lipstick, you still look completely fuckable."

"I'm sorry, *what?*"

"I said you look fuckable—"

"I heard you the first time, dude. You're not making any sense and causing offense isn't going to get you anywhere."

His eyes hardened, a darkly sexual look coming to the fore. "I don't mean any offense, but it's the truth. You look like the spawn of Satan."

She lifted her chin and gave him a glare. "Thanks for noticing, but that doesn't explain anything."

His gaze slid down her body before lifting to her face again. "You're appropriate for what I need because you're the epitome of *inappropriate*."

Angie couldn't keep her confusion from coming through. "Huh?"

"You look like the devil's daughter and yet you're sexy as fuck. Absolutely inappropriate for a man like me."

"*Right.*" Angie drew out the word on a breath, a tiny curl of both excitement and disappointment coiling in her belly. "I admit I'm a little out of my element here." She sucked in a breath. "I don't know what the hell you want, I don't even know your last name, but I'm pretty damn sure you're insulting me."

"I don't mean to be insulting." He paused a moment, contemplating her. "We're from two different worlds—"

"Yeah, and I think we need to keep it that way," Angie answered shortly.

He continued as if he'd never been interrupted, "It would be totally believable that I'd be unable to resist you." His eyes ran over her once again and when they rose to hers, she saw a warning reflected there. "Totally false, but nonetheless, believable." He pushed away from where he stood and took the five steps that separated them, holding out his hand.

Very carefully, Angie put her hand in his and her palm was promptly enclosed within a firm, sinewy handshake. "Damian Rule."

Angie licked her lips as both trepidation and excitement rushed down her spine. "Angie Ross."

"Nice to formally meet you, sweetheart. Can you spare me some time? There's a restaurant down the road and I promise I won't keep you out long."

Angie absolutely knew she should decline; nothing good could come from a meeting between them. He was insulting, antagonistic, and far too appealing for his own good. But the reason that she knew she was going to agree was simple. She was curious. She was *dying* to know what the hell he wanted.

She shrugged her shoulders and named the closest restaurant with an attached bar that she figured he'd appreciate.

"Yeah, that's the one," he agreed to her choice.

She pulled her hand from his. "I'll meet you there."

※※

Damian snagged a booth in the corner and held himself rigidly as he waited for Goth girl to arrive. She came in five minutes behind him, and although courtesy dictated that he stand at her entrance, his very noticeable physical reaction to her wouldn't allow him to move from his seat.

It was a knee-jerk reaction that he was going to have to get a handle on; surely time spent with her would lessen her physical appeal. He certainly had no plans to do anything about it. He wasn't going to sleep with her. *He. Was. Not.* He needed a business arrangement with her, and he couldn't sully that with an exchange of bodily fluids, no matter how hard she made him.

She slid in the seat across from him and didn't mince words. "What's up?"

"I've already ordered a drink, what do you want?"

She glanced from him and looked at the male waiter who'd come to her side. Damian felt the immediate loss of connection when she broke eye contact. As she turned a megawatt smile on the new arrival, Damian experienced a hot rush of anger, even as he took a forceful hit to his equilibrium, his senses stunned by the beauty that transformed her face. *He wanted that smile for himself.*

"I'll have a Diet Coke, please," she addressed the other man in a tone so feminine and pleasant that Damian clenched his fists.

The waiter stared at her for a moment too long by Damian's estimation, and when the younger man turned away, Damian tried to get a grip as he studied her. "You don't think you should have something stronger?"

She raised a single, perfect eyebrow. "Will I need something stronger?"

"No. Just thought we could make this easier by sharing a drink."

"Anesthesia by alcohol? Not tonight, thanks. I have to drive and I haven't had much to eat today."

After the drinks were placed in front of them, Damian requested two menus. He wasn't hungry, but she very obviously was.

When they were alone again, he studied her stiffened shoulders and attempted to put her at ease by admitting to his earlier lie. "You didn't mess up my hair."

She studied the menu and didn't bother to glance up. "No shit. Why'd you say that in the first place?"

"It was a reaction. You looked ready to bolt and I thought it would keep you in place for a few seconds more."

Her eyes flew to his and she asked neutrally, "What do you want with me?"

He declined to answer her question yet. "I hope you order something. I don't like knowing I'm holding you up from your supper."

She held his gaze for a second and then glanced at the menu once more. The waiter appeared again and she ordered an appetizer.

"Is that all you want?" Damian asked. The small helping wouldn't be enough to keep a bird alive.

"Are you going to eat half?" she accused.

"I might," he said, as the vision of sharing her food hit him as being particularly sensual.

She looked back to the waiter. "I'll have the grilled chicken and vegetable medley."

After the man turned to go, Damian tamped down his arousal and attempted to get down to business. "I need your help Saturday evening. Are you free?"

Her eyes narrowed to suspicious slits. "What kind of help?"

"I need a date for a dinner party."

The girl was smart; Damian could see her adding up the few things he'd already let slip and coming up with, if not his entire reason, then at least part of it.

She folded her arms over her chest and leaned back in her chair. It seemed as if she was attempting a casual look, but Damian wasn't buying it. Her voice was flat as she stated, "A woman like me is inappropriate for a businessman such as yourself," she restated his opinion in a controlled voice and then continued, "and yet someone needs to believe you're seriously interested in me."

Damian inclined his head minutely. "Correct so far."

"Who are you trying to fool?"

The girl was good; she caught on quickly. "We're trying to fool my mother."

She shook her head slightly and let out a half-smile. "There is no 'we.' I haven't agreed to anything."

"I'll pay you for your time," he offered abruptly.

"You'd *have* to pay me for my time. Saturday is my most lucrative day at the salon and I don't want to cut it short."

"A thousand dollars now and a thousand when the evening is over."

"*Holy shit.* Two grand just for a dinner party?" Distrust highlighted her features. "Nothing else?"

"Just a dinner party. Nothing else, although it has to look as if we can't wait to be alone. That is, if you think you're up to the challenge."

The first thing he saw was calculation as she very obviously thought about earning two grand in a single evening for little to no work. The second thing he saw was a question as she slid her gaze over him as if mulling over being alone with him. Damian felt the immediate hit to his groin as he imagined the same. It wasn't hard to do; being alone with her was something he thought about often. Her lips slowly opened and her face was transformed into a highly provocative look that made his pants too tight. Her voice came out, almost sultry and nothing like he'd heard from her before, "I'm pretty sure I could fake a bunch of people into thinking I'm into you."

He watched, almost entranced, as she lifted a hand and picked up a lock of hair and began twirling it around her fingers, and held the strand close to her mouth, making it impossible for him not to focus on her full lips. It was an obvious bid for sexual attention; it was also more than obvious that she was staging a performance, and damn if she wasn't good. She shrugged a delicate shoulder and continued, "I suppose for two grand I could manage to pretend you're not a complete douche bag for a few hours."

Damian raised an eyebrow. Her words themselves had been insulting, but the way she'd purred them had made it seem as if she couldn't wait to strip the clothes from his body...with her teeth. Yeah, if she could keep that up, she'd do just fine. His mother would buy it, hook, line and sinker. She'd finally get the message that he didn't have a single romantic feeling for Courtney and leave him alone again.

"So you'll do it?" he asked.

"Sure, why not?"

Damian was pleased he was getting what he wanted, although he acknowledged that he didn't care for how mercenary the girl seemed. Her tone had changed quickly when two grand was mentioned. It was a turn-off, but that was actually a good thing, because he needed something to dull the sharp edge of attraction he felt when he was near her.

He pulled out his business card and took a moment to jot down his cell phone number before handing it to her. "My information. I'll have a car pick you up at six sharp on Saturday night. Call and leave your information with my secretary. If you need to speak to me personally, call my cell."

"What do you want me to wear?"

"Something like that, of course," he said, indicating the outfit she had on.

She narrowed her eyes and a look of confusion colored them. "Umm, the party will be fairly formal, right? Or is it just us and your mother?"

"No, her dinner parties are usually twelve to sixteen guests."

She took a deep breath. "Right. I need to wear a cocktail dress at least, I think."

"Okay. But make it black and don't tone down the gothic element."

"All right, but I have to warn you that a dressed-up look will appear more polished."

"Black hair and purple lipstick?"

"If that's what you want," she agreed tonelessly.

"It is.

The car that picked Angie up on Saturday night had one thing she wasn't expecting: Damian in the backseat. For whatever reason, she'd thought she was meant to meet him at the party.

As she settled next to him, she tried to ignore the fact that he was studying her intently. Trying to calm her nerves, she attempted to focus on earning the money that would help Janice get out of the situation she was in.

She busied herself with the seatbelt and when he didn't speak and the car was in motion, she leaned back in her seat. When she continued to feel his hot eyes moving over her body, she flattened her palms against the leather and challenged, "You like what you see?"

His jaw tensed, his shoulders filling his jacket. "Most definitely. And that's the reason you're here."

"Because your mother has to believe this?"

He tipped his head in affirmation, his features giving nothing away.

She swallowed hard and tried to ignore the pounding in her chest that was induced by sitting so close to him. "So what's the story?"

"There is no 'story.' All we'll need is the complete truth, except for the part about the payment you're receiving."

"Okay." She cleared her throat and demanded an answer to the question that had been bothering her since she'd agreed to this scheme. "There won't be any PDAs, will there?"

For a moment he wore a blank look and then he smiled wickedly, his straight white teeth solidifying the perfection of his smile. "Public displays of affection?"

She exhaled, trying to remember exactly why she couldn't risk the intimacy of touches between them. "Yeah."

A frown came between his brows. "I shouldn't think so." His expression stilled and became grave. "I'm assuming you want me to relinquish you after this night is over, correct?"

Caught off guard by his intimation, her stomach dropped to her feet, but she managed to nod her head, her eyes glued to his.

At her non-verbal confirmation, he answered brusquely, "Then no, no unnecessary touching." Negating his words, he reached out a hand and lifted her chin, tipping her face up to his. Her nerves shifting restlessly, Angie tried to suppress the pleasure his touch created within her. "You clean up quite well, but

I distinctly remember requesting the gothic look," he said in a voice that contained irritation and a hint of accusation.

Her heart pounded in her chest as his hand slid back and forth over her cheek, the pads of his fingers feeling rough and supremely masculine. It took every ounce of brainpower Angie had left to concentrate on the conversation. "This was as gothic as I could make it and still retain my dignity. I'm twenty-seven, not seventeen." Her breath hitched as his fingers tightened on her skin and she had to force her vocal chords to continue working. "Black dress, sheer black stockings, black hair and nails. What more did you want?"

His eyes dropped to her mouth and lingered before snapping back up and blasting her with a hard, implacable expression. "I distinctly remember requesting the purple lipstick."

As the tantalizing scent of his after-shave rushed over her, she shook her head. "It just didn't work with the dress," she said softly.

"I'm paying you two-thousand dollars. I want the purple lip color. Do you have it in your bag?"

She did. She'd thrown it in, just in case. "Yes."

"Put it on," he grunted, his finger sliding over her bottom lip.

Angie fumbled with the clasp of her tiny black shoulder bag and withdrew the lipstick, fighting her nerves the entire time. His hand dropped away and she popped the top from the tube and began to apply the loud, obnoxious color. She needed no mirror; her stepmother-at-the-time had taught her how to apply lipstick without one when she was a teenager, telling her that it was something every woman should know how to do in a pinch. It was difficult with fingers that were trembling, but when it was accomplished, Angie looked back to him.

His gaze sharpened as he studied her, a dangerous glint highlighting his eyes as they roved over her. His lips flattened as if he were pissed about something and the blood pumped furiously in her veins as he hissed out, "Yeah, you're as sexy as fuck."

Her pulse quickening erratically, Angie watched, as if in a trance, as he pulled a silk handkerchief from his pocket and began wiping at her lips, dragging the material back and forth over her skin until she knew there couldn't be a trace of color left. When he was finished he sat back, his stare bold and assessing. Angie struggled to form words. "Why did you do that?"

At the same moment she acknowledged that she was dying for his touch, he spoke in a gravelly voice, "You were right. It doesn't work. There's sexy…and then there's sexy. You don't need any help and I don't need the complication."

Her heart dropped in disappointment even as she knew that he was right. He might not need the complication, but she damn sure didn't need someone like him in her life. Even *if* the thought of going to bed with him was so tempting it was sending a river of longing through her bloodstream.

The car pulled up to a house awash in lights and movement. The atmosphere seemed convivial, and they hadn't even stepped from the vehicle yet. She ran her hands down her skirt and attempted to get her unruly emotions under control.

Angie gripped her champagne glass with fingers that trembled. She listened with only half an ear to the conversation going on around her.

She realized immediately that this had been a mistake. It was more than obvious that Damian's mother was trying to set him up with the young woman who'd been introduced to Angie as Courtney Powell.

When they'd first arrived ten minutes before, Mrs. Rule had appeared crestfallen when she'd seen Angie with her son.

As she'd led them around, Damian's mother had introduced the younger woman to Angie as 'my goddaughter and Damian's dear, dear friend,' and Angie had absorbed the not-so-subtle hint that her son was already taken.

Expecting to dislike this Courtney girl for a reason she couldn't quite figure out, Angie had been surprised that the girl seemed quite nice. When they'd been introduced, there had been an obvious look of relief on the younger girl's face when she'd realized that Damian had brought a date. She'd given Angie a smile that contained real warmth.

But his mother certainly appeared to be disappointed and Angie experienced a sudden guilt that she hadn't expected to feel at the subterfuge.

Now, as she stood in the middle of the living room of this 'mini-mansion', Angie sipped champagne and tried to hold up her end of the conversation, while her hostess gently interrogated her. Damian had been pulled away by a man she assumed was a business acquaintance, and he stood across the room in a larger circle of guests that included Courtney. His mother had manipulated that, and Angie could see by the tense line of his jaw that her move had angered him. He didn't seem to be annoyed with the younger girl, just…oblivious. But still, Angie couldn't help but feel a bit sorry for her, even though it had been apparent to Angie that the other girl didn't want his attention.

Angie stood rooted to the floor, knowing damn good and well that she shouldn't have agreed to this. She began counting down the hours until the evening ended and she could disappear from these people's lives just as quickly as she'd come onto the scene. If it hadn't been for Janice and this seemingly simple way to grab some fast cash for her friend, Angie would never have agreed to the scheme.

"What do you do, dear?" Damian's mother asked as the man to the immediate left of Angie listened in on the conversation and inched just a tad too close for her liking.

"I'm a hairdresser." She took another sip and attempted a smile as she tried to discreetly edge away from the man without drawing attention.

"You own your own salon?" The older woman asked.

"No." Angie named the shop where she worked, although she was very sure these people didn't even know it existed, much less where it was located.

"And that's where you met my son?" she asked with no apparent animosity.

"Yes, ma'am." Angie forced the smile to stay on her lips as she wiped away a drop of condensation from her glass.

"Your make-up is quite unusual." The older woman looked her over curiously, but not in a rude way, to Angie's relief.

"Thank you, I guess. It suits me."

"Why yes, it does. And I did mean it as a compliment. You're very beautiful," Mrs. Rule said in a softly sincere tone.

Well, that was sweetly put. Angie knew for a fact that she wasn't beautiful, but how could she not like this woman for pretending that she was? After her earlier surprise when she'd found out her son hadn't come alone, the older woman had done nothing but try to make Angie feel welcome. What was it exactly that Damian was hoping to accomplish with this ruse? "Thank you. I love your dress." Angie had never been one for small talk, and she hoped she didn't sound awkward.

"Oh, this old thing?" Mrs. Rule slid her hands down the folds of her dress. "It's one of my favorites."

Angie glanced around the beautifully decorated room. "You have a lovely home."

"Thank you so much, sweetheart. I love this old house; it's where we raised our children."

Angie ran her eyes swiftly over the room. The house might be old, but it was immaculately decorated and updated. She took a sip of champagne and latched onto the topic she was sure would keep the other woman talking, so she herself wouldn't have to. "How many children do you have?"

"One daughter who's my youngest, Erin. She couldn't be here tonight. And three sons. Nick lives in the city although he told me he couldn't make it tonight, either," she said with an expression that Angie couldn't read. "And my youngest son, Garrett, is out of the country. But, of course, Courtney is here and she's like a daughter to me as well."

"You guys must be very close then," Angie said, not knowing how to reply and wondering for a brief moment what it must have been like for Damian to have grown up with so many siblings. She herself was an only child and having a sibling was something that she missed when she had time to think about it.

"Well, I've raised her since she was seventeen. Her mother was my best friend."

"I'm so sorry," Angie said, not really knowing how to respond, as an anguished look crossed the other woman's face. It held so much pain that Angie assumed the girl had been orphaned. She glanced away to give her hostess a second to regain her composure.

As her eyes landed across the room, Angie noticed a tall man enter from a side door. He looked around, as if he were taking in everything the room held with a single glance. She sucked in a breath as she recognized his undeniable resemblance to Damian.

Once Mrs. Rule regained her composure and began talking about her youngest son and his travels, Angie surreptitiously watched as the newcomer slid behind Courtney on silent feet and wrapped his fingers around her wrist. The younger girl's face paled as she froze in place but didn't move, and the man, unquestionably one of Damian's brothers, leaned down and whispered something close to her ear. The girl's face drained of all color and then immediately filled with heat, and before

Angie could make out anything more, the man abruptly pulled her from the room.

The maneuver was accomplished so quickly and silently that Angie doubted anyone else had noticed. Damian didn't appear to realize that the woman who'd been standing next to him was no longer there as he continued conversing with the men around him.

Mrs. Rule excused herself to check on dinner, and immediately, the man who'd been hovering next to Angie zeroed in on her, making her hackles rise. He slid his slimy gaze up and down her body and her stomach curdled in reaction. "So, you cut hair for a living?" he questioned in a pretentious, nasally tone.

Angie took an obvious step back from him. "Yeah."

His eyes gleamed, making her feel a bit more nauseated. "Do you give massages too?"

Angie never had time to form an answer or, for that matter, feel insulted. An arm snaked around her waist from behind as she was pulled into a hard, warm body that had about as much give as finely tempered steel. "Robertson," Damian hissed under his breath. "I don't believe I care for your tone or your question."

Angie saw the blood drain from the other man's face as he took a step back. "I didn't mean anything by it."

"No?" Damian bit out.

"I was only trying to make conversation."

The harsh look on Damian's features made a lie of the congenial nod he gave. "You know, I've never cared for you. I've put up with you only because my mother seems to enjoy your company." Angie felt his fingers tighten on her waist as his words turned menacing. "But all bets are off if you attempt, *in any way*, to fuck with my girl here. You insult her one more time, you'll find yourself without a friend in this city so fast it'll make your head spin. You get me, man?"

The other man's face turned a whiter shade of pale. "Yeah."

Robertson turned and fled the room, and Angie was left semi-alone with Damian, his arm still wrapped around her. She swallowed and tried to digest the scene that had just taken place. "Wow," she said as she turned toward him, facing him while his other arm came around to enclose her entirely within his grasp. "And I thought that I could act." She tapped him on the shoulder, because she was floored and didn't know what else to do. "That was amazing."

He stared down at her for a moment too long and Angie felt her insides turn to mush. His voice when he answered was deep and sure. "That wasn't acting." He shook his head as if to clear it. "I don't know what the fuck it was, but it wasn't acting."

With that, he grabbed her by the hand and led her into the dining room to join the others who were congregating there.

Chapter Three

The limo pulled in front of her apartment and idled, the privacy screen drawn up to provide a seclusion that Angie wasn't quite comfortable with. The rest of the evening had been long and tedious, only because Angie's nerves were affected. After the scene with the Robertson guy, the party had sailed smoothly with everyone else accepting her and including her as if she were one of them.

And now, as they sat in the back of the car, the payment had already been made, and even though it had made her uneasy to take it, she knew she'd had to.

She pasted on a smile and held out her hand, determined to give Damian a business-like shake before she went inside. "Well, good-bye."

He glanced down with a maddening hint of arrogance, his gaze riveted on her face before dropping to examine every inch of her. Something intense flared between them and her heart jolted, the prolonged anticipation of his touch almost unbearable. Slowly, he put his palm against hers, wrapping his fingers around her hand, squeezing, but not letting go. "Are you planning on escaping with a handshake?" His voice was deep yet smooth, melting her insides where she sat.

Her pulse pounded and she could barely form a word when she thought about what he might be inferring. "Yes?" The word that should have been an affirmation sounded like a question, even to her own ears.

He frowned as if he couldn't fathom that she might want to escape from him. "After all those hot little looks you gave me from across the dinner table?"

He'd given *her* hot looks all evening as well, and even now, the expression on his face was both seductive and filled with virile appeal. "I thought that's what you wanted from me. You said it had to look real."

His steady gaze bore into her, making her stomach tingle. "You went far beyond what I expected, though."

Was it apparent to him that any acting on her part hadn't been necessary? Mortification filled her and she attempted to divert him from the truth. "I'm sorry. I've never taken acting classes or anything. I was flying by the seat of my pants."

"Yeah, but now for the sixty-four thousand dollar question." He slid a single finger down her cheek. "Was it all an act?"

The smoldering flame in his eyes was beginning to panic her. This would *so not* be a good idea, no matter what the tingle between her thighs was telling her. "What...what do you mean?"

"Your hot little looks indicated you wanted nothing more than to get me naked." He glanced up from her lips and his eyes caught and captured hers. "Is that the way it is or did I misread you?"

Damn. "Um..."

"It would be good, you know?"

Jesus, he smelled good. Concentrate, Angie. "Yeah, but it wouldn't be a *good idea*," she managed to say, her eyes glued to his.

"I agree with you." Angie's heart almost stopped when his fingers dropped to the top swell of her breast. Without looking away from her eyes, his thumb flicked just once against her nipple and she froze. "It's a bad idea." His gaze dropped to her breast as he hissed out, *"It's a fucked-up idea."*

Angie attempted to maintain control though it was all but impossible; her heart was racing so fast she could barely speak. "Bad idea…nothing in common," she rattled.

"I wouldn't go that far." His palm enclosed her breast entirely and he squeezed just hard enough that the immediate pleasure she felt was enhanced by a tiny frisson of pain. His gaze lifted and stayed riveted to her eyes as he rasped, "We have one thing in common." He squeezed again, his thumb spearing across her nipple. "We want to fuck each other so badly we can hardly stand it."

Angie attempted to rear back from him but he wrapped his beefy fist around her upper arm. "Not so fast. We're only talking. You can take that frightened look off your face." The blood rushed through her veins making her light-headed but she didn't attempt to get away again.

"I'm not frightened."

"No?" He looked doubtful.

She shook her head.

"The fact that I want to take you home and strip you butt-assed naked and sink into you from behind doesn't scare you? Not even a little bit?"

Angie was held spellbound, unable to answer as the descriptive image caused wet heat to pool between her thighs.

His eyes ran over her lips before clashing with hers again. "Doesn't the fact that I have a hunger for you that makes me want to restrain you to a flat surface and do obscene and salacious things to your body scare you?"

Oh. My. God. Angie couldn't tell if her pulse was pounding so quickly she couldn't feel it anymore or if it had stopped completely. "What...what kind of things?"

"Sweetheart, that's not a fair question if you're still planning on escaping unscathed tonight."

She felt the blood drain from her face. *She couldn't afford to get involved with this guy.* She had some kind of self-preservation reflex that was screaming at her to get out of the car. "Okay. Scratch that question."

༺༻

Leave it be, Rule.

You're playing with fire.

Getting back at the little witch with looks and innuendos was one thing.

Sinking his fingers around her breast and telling her exactly what he wanted was taking it one step too far; he was only punishing himself because he knew he couldn't have her. Sure, he could probably *have* her, but there was a goddamn pounding in his head that was warning him that once he'd had her, it would be far from simple to let her go. But hell, he couldn't seem to stop himself from making it worse. His damn hand was still wrapped around her breast, following the dictate of his cock, and his fucking mouth was on automatic pilot. "It's too late to scratch the question."

She blinked up at him; she was so close he could see the pulse pounding against the silky white column of her neck. Without taking his eyes from her, because he couldn't drag them away, he slid his hand from her breast and wrapped it around her throat, holding it there. He felt her pulse jump and quiver, saw her eyes close before opening again in panic. He felt his nostrils flare in response. Oh, yeah, he wanted to fuck her. He'd probably die if he couldn't. He *would* die, because he couldn't let himself have her.

He couldn't have her, but he couldn't stop from pressing against her throat, couldn't stop his mouth from falling to her ear. "Has anyone ever owned your body? Because that's how it would be between us." He bit her earlobe and sucked it into his mouth, savoring her taste, her scent, before continuing, "If you were mine, it would appear to the world as if you had a normal life, you might even feel as if your days were your own. But that would be an illusion; it wouldn't be just fucking with you and me. If you ever made the mistake of sleeping with me, it wouldn't be just sex. So, I'm warning you now. *I'd own you.* I'd own your body; I'd own your orgasms. I'd strip you naked, spread you wide and play with your body to my satisfaction before I'd ever let you experience release. Don't get me wrong, you wouldn't ever want to get away from me, but sweetheart, your life as you know it would be over. So before you ever let me sweet talk you into bed, understand that I'm just a little bit insane when it comes to you. It's the reason I've never put a move on you before, and it's the reason I'm going to let you slip away untouched tonight. I'm going to try my fucking best to stay away from you, but I don't know how long I'll be able to manage it. So if I come at you sometime in the future lying through my teeth and telling you it'll only be for fun, don't you fucking believe me. So, consider this the only warning you're going to get. I'm going to let you run from me tonight, but before you go, I have to taste you."

Damian slid away from her ear and fastened his mouth to her lips and took the kiss he needed to retain his sanity. Her lips were soft and trembling; he tried to be gentle but had no clue if he was succeeding. If this was the only kiss he would be allowed, he needed to make it count. He pushed inside; she tasted like the sweetest drug. He imagined kissing her between her thighs, putting his tongue there and tasting the magic he knew he'd find.

She mewled in his arms and his grasp became tighter. Her scent was sending a scorching need through his veins, his cock was hard, pulsing blood in a cadence that was screaming at him to pull her skirt up and rip her underwear aside. His abdominal muscles tightened in pure lust; she was everything he'd ever fantasized about. *More.* She was more. She was dragging oxygen into her lungs in rapid inhalations, and he felt a growl erupt from his throat at the same moment he shoved his hand up her skirt.

He found stockings. Thigh-high stockings that wouldn't impede him in the slightest. He pushed his tongue deep into the recesses of her mouth and then pulled it out again. *"Want to fuck you."* His words were guttural. He invaded her mouth again, as his hand found the tiny triangle that covered her feminine heat. Even through the thin layer of material, he could tell that she was completely slick and smooth. Waxed. Clean-shaven. It was so fucking erotic that he had to clench his muscles in order to retain control. He tried to keep his touch light and teasing because he refused to scare her, but he knew he was failing. It was taking everything he had to go slow, but he could feel the subtle tensing of her muscles and knew he had to be careful. He maneuvered her knees further apart, pulled the flimsy material away from the wet core he *needed* to sink into and positioned his middle finger at her entrance, ready to impale her. He lifted away from her mouth and watched the expression on her face, waiting for her to open her eyes.

Angie's nerves shifted when she felt her knees shoved apart and her panties pushed roughly aside. Her eyes flew open and she found him staring down at her. "I thought…I thought we weren't going to do this."

"Not going to fuck. Not going to screw you. Just have to feel you." Angie vaguely recognized that his usual urbane method of speech had fallen by the wayside and that he was grunting like a caveman. She was barely cognizant of anything except for the thick, blunt finger swirling around her opening, teasing her.

She couldn't let him.

Against her will, her world was filled with lights as a sharp arrow of pleasure pierced through her and her eyes closed with a volition of their own.

She knew she only had a second or two before he plunged inside, and against everything her body was screaming for, she reached between them and gripped his hand in denial. He hissed out a flat sound that threatened repercussion, but after an abbreviated, tension-filled moment, he let her control the movement of his hand long enough to lift it away from her body by a degree. The sharp hold he had on the material lessened just enough that her panties snapped back into place, covering her.

Her eyes flew open and they stared at each other, breathing deeply. She loosened her hold on his hand just enough that, instantaneously, it went back to her feminine center, and he began touching her over the material of her underwear, and within seconds, her panties were completely damp.

Her flimsy underwear offered little protection; his touch felt almost as good as it had before the material created a barrier between them. His eyes held hers, sharp and assessing, refusing to let her look away from him. Her reaction was swift and violent. Sexual arousal held her in its grip and she began moving against his hand in a subtle motion that she tried to control, but it was enough that it brought her to the edge so quickly that it almost panicked her.

His fingers slid over the material in a provocative motion, they slid over the slit that concealed her wet opening, to her clit and then back again. His teeth gritted, the words rattling from his throat in a disjointed sentence that reflected his struggle for control. *"Make you come like this."*

The words scared the living shit out of her. They scared the arousal straight from her body. She slammed her eyes closed again, shutting him out. She didn't want him to make her come. It was too soon, too intimate, *way too intimate*, and she didn't know him or trust him enough to let him see her without any control. She hurtled back to earth as she stiffened under him.

He must have felt her withdrawal because his hand tightened on her momentarily before releasing her. With icy precision, he reached up and fisted his hand in her hair. She opened her mouth to try to speak, but closed it again as she was silenced by his dark, purely frustrated expression. Her heart beat loudly in her ears as his features turned brooding.

He held her tightly, and whether he was testing himself or her, she didn't know. His control seemed to be on a knife edge, it could go either way, and she held herself perfectly still, wanting to run and flee, but longing to stay within the irresistible prison of his arms for a few seconds more. She exhaled a shallow pant as a shiver of response ran down her spine as he continued to stare at her with a look of barely-concealed lustful intent.

With a hungry hiss escaping from his chest, his hand dropped to her breast. Angie's face paled, thinking it was about to start all over again.

He felt her defensive reaction and snarled deep in his throat as he released her breast. *"Fuck."*

He lifted his hand from her hair and sat back, his jaw clenching tightly as he looked away and stared out the window. He took several deep breaths and cracked his knuckles. *"Goodnight."* The word was rough.

Angie sucked in a breath as disappointment and relief mingled within. She looked at him with a question in her eyes as she hastily pushed her skirt below her knees.

He turned back to face her. "Go on. Get out of the car."

Angie reared back from the harsh demand and put her hand on the door handle, but still she hesitated, even though she didn't understand why.

His muscles tightened and his nostrils flared. "You remember my warning?" His eyes narrowed, almost threateningly. "You best get out of the car, Angie, while I'm giving you the chance."

She watched him for the space of three seconds, apprehension rioting within her, and then she took the advice she was given, opened the door and fled.

※

A week later, Damian silently castigated himself as his hair was being cut. What. The. *Hell?* What the fuck was wrong with him that he couldn't stay away from this place? He could have easily gone another week before getting a haircut to begin with, but coming here again? He needed his fucking head examined.

The hairdresser, Janice, was exceptionally talkative today, and although he tried to drown her out with his thoughts as he looked around for the little witch, he couldn't help but hear at least half of what she said.

"So, anyway, I can't thank you enough."

His eyes snapped back to hers. "I'm sorry, what?"

"Thank you for the money. I mean, I realize that it actually came from Angie, but you gave it to her, and without the generosity from both of you, I'd still be in a fix. I can't tell you what it means to me. I'm sure Angie told you about the situation my ex left me and my daughter in."

As she rattled on and on, Damian could focus on only one thing. *Goth girl* hadn't kept the money for herself. She'd given it to her friend, making any disparaging thoughts he may have had about her mercenary ways, false.

He gritted his teeth. He wanted to think of her as mercenary. He *needed* to think of her as grasping and avaricious. He didn't care for women who were greedy. In fact, he could now admit that he might have had an underlying reason for giving her the money and setting up the date to begin with. He'd *wanted* to think badly of her.

But now she'd gone and fucked that up for him. Instead of being greedy, she'd proven herself to be caring and unselfish.

Shit. It pissed him off just thinking about it.

Another nail in his coffin.

※

Angie finished her sandwich and glanced up from wiping down the counters in the small kitchenette.

Her stomach plummeted to her feet as Damian crowded the doorway. He glanced to the right and then to the left before focusing his attention on her with inflexible intent. He took a step forward, and she watched in appalled horror as he both slammed the door and then turned and locked it, trapping her inside the small room with him.

"What the hell do you think you're doing?" The screech came from her throat even as she tried to sound composed. "You can't be in here."

"I think you're wrong." He lifted his hands with supreme arrogance to indicate his location. "You see me, right?"

"Did you have an appointment?"

He crossed his arms over his chest. "Why else would I be here if I didn't?"

His hair did look newly trimmed. "You can't be back here," she repeated, dumbstruck.

"I have a problem with you that we need to discuss."

The look in his eyes raised her hackles and she backed up until her spine touched the counter and she couldn't go any farther. "What'd I do now?" She'd tried, every minute of every day since she'd gotten out of his car, not to think of him, but it was an impossible task.

"You gave away the money," he accused.

Angie narrowed her eyes as she attempted to understand what his problem with that could be. "So? It was my money, right? You gave it to me, and I gave it to Janice."

"You shouldn't have done that," he said in a voice that promised retribution.

"Why? She needed it more than I did."

For whatever reason, her comment appeared to land like a hit to his upper torso as Angie saw him actually flinch. He remained silent but took several steps forward until he stood just beyond her comfort zone. She sucked in a breath and steeled her nerves. "Look, I'm sorry if you wanted me to spend it on...a more suitable wardrobe or whatever, but it was my understanding it was mine, to do with as I pleased."

His generously curved lips parted in a snarl. "It was yours. But you were supposed to want it for yourself."

All at once, Angie thought she understood. "Oh. Okay. You thought I was a greedy little bitch and now you're pissed to find out that I'm not. Well, that's too damn bad." A flare of temper hardened her voice and every curve of her body radiated defiance, "So you can leave now."

He didn't move a single muscle. Unless you counted the tic flaring in his cheek, he was absolutely still as he watched her, like an animal ready to pounce. The accusation in his eyes was menacing, sinister even, but the sexual threat that lay just underneath the surface had Angie hyperventilating.

As she stood rooted to the floor, he came another two steps closer and lifted his hand toward her hair. He did so very slowly, as if giving her a chance to rebuff his advance, and when she became too paralyzed to move, his fingers landed in her hair and spiked through her tresses, holding her scalp within his palm. As he held her hostage, he leaned down and bit at her bottom lip, just a tiny bite, but it reflected his impatience, and it sent currents of thrilling heat radiating through her bloodstream.

She closed her eyes against him, and when she did, his hand tightened on her scalp and his arm wrapped around her waist. "Yeah, you were supposed to be greedy," he said with anger. *"I don't like greedy women."*

Her eyes flew open to find him staring down at her, his nostrils flaring. His belligerent words struck her in the heart. "Douche bag," she bit out.

A ferocious look crossed his features and he looked as if he wanted to shake her, but he didn't. "Not. Nice," he bit back, and if possible, his hands turned even more vise-like.

"Too damn bad if you don't like it. You're not the boss of me; you don't tell me how to act."

"I don't give a shit about being the boss of you. I don't want to tell you how to act. All. I. Want. Is. To. *Fuck. You.*"

She took a quick intake of breath and ignored the tingle between her legs. "Too bad. You're an ass. A fucking—"

Her words were cut off when his mouth swept down onto hers and every thought in her head splintered as heat, an amazing heat slid down her spine and coalesced within her veins. A great wave of pleasure inundated every cell in her body, a feeling unlike any she'd ever experienced exploding within and consuming her in its entirety. Her blood began pumping rapidly as his arms held her imprisoned, her femininity no match against his masculine virility as he held her with a barely suppressed

47

violence that excited her so much she could barely manage to breathe.

Angie gave herself approximately ten seconds to enjoy his kiss, *maybe* twenty, *possibly thirty,* and then she slid her arms between them and began pushing against him. His chest was like a solid wall of iron, with no give at all, and her fingers spread out over his muscles, testing his strength and trying without much success to force herself to step away from him.

He must have felt her conflicting emotions and he lifted his head, his eyes dilating before focusing on her. A tinge of red colored his cheekbones, and the fervor reflected in his eyes both fascinated her and threatened her ability to stand on her own two feet. When he spoke, his voice was gruff. "I may be an ass, but it's *your fault.* If you weren't so *fucking beautiful,* maybe you wouldn't have my head so fucked-up." As he spoke, the arm that held her slid down and his fingers grabbed the fleshy part of her butt and squeezed, sending new currents of electric heat along her spine. "It would be good, angel," he said, self-assuredly. "What time do you get off?"

Abruptly his question bled through her messed-up brain-waves, and she realized what he was asking her. "What time do I get off? *That's it?* Where's the sweet talk?" His arrogance and conceit knew no bounds. As she waited for his answer, Angie admitted she wasn't in any danger of falling in love with him, but she was captivated by his irrefutable strength and masculinity; she knew she shouldn't be, but she was. The window for imposing her will was narrowing, she could feel herself literally falling under his spell as she wondered for the zillionth time what it would be like to go to bed with him. She *ached* to sleep with him, and that exasperated the hell out of her. How in the hell could she want to sleep with somebody she didn't even like?

His eyes narrowed in confusion. "Sweet talk?"

"You warned me that you might try to sweet talk me into bed. What? You can't even be bothered with that?"

He shrugged a shoulder but made no attempt to release her. "Okay. How's this?" A frown of concentration came between his brows. "You're gorgeous and it wouldn't be just for me. I could get you off, too, baby."

As his words sank in, Angie began pushing against him. "Oh, my God." He let her go after a minute pause and she paced across the small room before turning to face him. "You're unbelievable."

"What exactly do you want me to say?" he asked, modulating the question evenly.

She began shaking her head in denial. "Nothing. Nothing at all."

He crossed his arms over his chest, and when he spoke, his words were edged with steel. "You're only denying the inevitable."

Angie rolled her eyes and began shaking her head. "Yeah, *I don't think so.*"

"You think you can stay away from me?" His question contained a hint of laughter, an arrogant boastfulness.

"Well, it's probably going to be hard, what with your silver tongue and all, but I'm going to give it a shot."

"You're making fun of me," he said with a frown.

"Little bit, yeah."

"You think this is funny?" His tone, though controlled, suddenly held an ominous quality.

"Not really. Just not interested." Angie bit her lip. She had no idea how she managed to tell such a bold-faced lie.

He studied her a moment in controlled silence, myriad expressions crossing his features. "We'll see." With that, he turned and walked out and only when he'd left the building, could Angie begin breathing normally again.

A few days later, Angie finished up a haircut and castigated herself for not being able to concentrate as usual. The episode with Damian Rule had screwed up her ability to go on as usual; she didn't know why, but she felt different. His challenge that she wouldn't be able to stay away from him was messing her up on the inside, and suddenly, every man she saw on the street or came into contact with at the salon, she compared with him. And much to her annoyance, every one of them came up lacking. As she swept up around her station after her last customer, the receptionist, a girl called Amber, came up to her. "There's a lady who wants to see you."

"Who is it?" Angie asked, wishing she had a few minutes before her next appointment to calm her nerves.

"I didn't ask." The girl went back to the front of the salon and Angie followed her. Much to her shock, Damian's mother slid to her feet and before Angie could catch her breath, the older woman enveloped her in a warm hug.

"Surprised to see me?"

Surprise didn't begin to cover it. Think of the devil and his mother appears. "Sure am. How are you, Mrs. Rule?"

"I'm well, darling. I was in the neighborhood and thought I'd come check out your little shop. It's nice." She glanced around, smiling. "Do you have time to sneak out for a while? I'd love to take you to lunch and we can have a nice, long chat."

A chat? Um, no. "I wish I could, but I'm working straight through. I've got appointments lined up all afternoon."

The older woman's face fell. "Oh, poo. That's too bad. Maybe I'll make an appointment and you can do my hair next week. I'm looking for someone new, anyway. That way we'll have plenty of time to talk."

"That sounds wonderful." *That so did not sound wonderful.* Angie grabbed a card from the reception desk and handed it to her. "Call anytime. I'd be honored to do your hair."

"Can we set it up now?"

"Umm," Angie faltered, "I don't see why not." *Damn it.*

She grabbed the appointment book and they quickly agreed on a date and time and then the other woman gave her a swift hug and began to leave. But before Angie could breathe a sigh of relief, the older woman stopped and said, "You're just as cute as a little button. I want you to know that it didn't take me long at all to realize that you'd be *perfect* for Damian. You look as if you're a spontaneous kind of girl, and that's exactly what my son needs in the rigid life he insists on leading."

Angie had no clue how to react or what to say and stumbled over her answer. "Thank you so much. I'll see you next week."

"I'll be here with bells on, darling."

Great. Just what Angie was afraid of.

On Angie's day off, she found herself standing in front of a large glass and steel building in the middle of downtown, staring up at it. She glanced back down at the business card Damian had given her and decided that she was definitely in the right place.

Had she made the correct decision to come here? That, she didn't know. She'd begun losing sleep from worrying about her appointment next week with his mother, and for the life of her, she couldn't figure out what to do about it. Should she tell him? Did he have a clue that instead of meeting her and looking at her with contempt, his mother seemed to actually like her?

And why hadn't she just picked up the phone and called him? It would have been so simple to give him a head's up about his mother's upcoming visit. But no, she hadn't done that. She was standing in front of his building, refusing to believe that the reason for it was because she couldn't stay away from him, just as he'd earlier challenged.

She could stay away from him if she wanted to. Of course she could. She couldn't be controlled by her libido, not if she didn't allow it.

But who was to say that she shouldn't allow herself to see him? Who really cared if he was right? This wasn't about who was right or who was wrong. She was caught up in her own emotions and this didn't have anything to do with reason.

She acknowledged that he was one of the most compelling men she'd ever met, and the spark of excitement she was experiencing just looking up at the building where he worked was filling her drab life with animation.

Her heart pounding an erratic rhythm, she straightened her spine and walked inside the glass doors.

Damian called 'enter' and glanced up as his secretary hovered just inside his doorway. "What exactly was it about *no interruptions* that you failed to understand?" He attempted to control the impatience in his tone but knew that he hadn't managed it.

She flinched and he felt a small sliver of guilt. He'd been out of sorts for a few weeks and didn't know what the hell was wrong with him. "I'm sorry, sir, but the situation seems a bit out of the ordinary."

"What exactly, seems out of the ordinary?"

"There's a woman here to see you—"

"How is that out of the ordinary?" Damian spit the words out. One of the reasons he'd given precise instructions was the amount of work he had scheduled and the random women who occasionally showed up at his office who attempted to stop him from accomplishing it.

"She has a card with your personal cell phone number, and she's...*different.*"

Damian's throat closed up and a tight coil of sexual tension consumed him. "What's her name?" he managed to ask, fighting his arousal at just the thought of the little witch coming to his office. *No need to bust a fuse, Rule, it won't be her.*

"Angela Ross."

Damian felt his temperature skyrocket. "Send her in." His abdominal muscles tightened. "And no interruptions while she's here. *Understand?* I don't care if the President of the United States calls. I don't care if the building catches fire. *No interruptions.*"

"Yes, sir." His secretary turned with visible relief and Damian stood up and walked around to the front of his desk, waiting for the little witch with ill-concealed impatience.

※※

Angie followed Damian's secretary across what seemed like miles of plush carpet and walked into the office when indicated. She was still in a state of shock; she'd found out in the reception area that he didn't merely work in the downtown high-rise, *he owned the building.*

She heard the door snap closed behind her, and with her heart catching, she faltered just inside the large room. Her gaze was caught and held by dark eyes as he leaned against a desk of solid mahogany while standing completely still, obviously awaiting her arrival. His eyes were both sharp and hooded, his body held in a pose of relaxation that seemed inconsistent with the almost tangible electricity that radiated from him in waves.

Her pulse pounding, her footsteps stalled completely. Before she could get a word out, he pushed off the desk and began to track her across the office, his muscles corded and his eyes reflecting a sheen of purpose. The space between them narrowed rapidly as his eyes fell to her throat and then scanned her body quickly before lifting to her face again.

Any semblance of a smile dissolved as his expression hardened imperceptibly; a raw sizzle filled the air as his brooding features reflected a harsh, atavistic hunger that almost brought Angie to her knees as he stood not six inches away in all his tall, masculine glory.

He stood almost indolently for the beat of three seconds before reaching out and seizing her with a dominant force that gave her not an ounce of choice in the matter. He mumbled two words, *"Thank fuck,"* in a guttural rasp that, had she realized it, contained an evocative foreshadowing of his future intent where she was concerned.

Chapter Four

The oxygen froze in Angie's lungs as she felt, with some annoyance at herself, his short pursuit closing around her as her blood sizzled with a desperate need to give in to him. He was too good-looking, too compelling, too commanding for her to keep refusing him. She'd already been through the arguments in her head; she wouldn't be able to come up with the necessary willpower to continue to deny what they both wanted. It was a heated debate she'd been having internally for days and days: *Stay away from him.* No. *He's bad for you.* I don't care. *You might get hurt.* I'll take the chance.

Her mind was in a convoluted frenzy as she stood frozen within his embrace. With the fingers of both hands wrapped around her upper arms, he jerked her forward until her upper torso clashed against the hard planes of his stomach. Immediate, potent awareness hit her in an arousal of need so powerful that she could barely breathe. His mouth swooped down to hers, and as she tried to stand upright, he propelled her backward until her spine was flattened against the door.

One brawny hand released her, and she heard the sibilant hiss of the lock being turned behind her. A delicious shudder of anticipation heated her blood. *This was not what she had come here for.* She looked up into fevered brown eyes staring down at her and felt seared by his potent magnetism. Her heartbeat hammering in her ears, she couldn't tell if the pulse she felt pumping came from his chest or hers. Her reaction to him was so swift and violent that she almost couldn't believe it. Certainly nothing in her past experience had come even remotely close to the overwhelming way that he made her feel.

Her eyes dropped to the base of his throat. It was tanned and laced with sinewy muscle, an obvious pulse showing where the blood pumped swiftly through his veins. He was invading her personal space as if it were his due; his legs were braced apart on either side of hers, holding her trapped. He pressed his body so closely against hers that she could feel his pulsing arousal. His erection against her was hard and hot and it inflamed her senses to a dangerous degree.

"Giving up so easily?" His voice was brusque and arrogant as he slid his free hand into her hair and lifted her face, controlling her easily, allowing her no movement to turn away from him, even had she wanted to.

His words brought her back to herself; she wasn't here to engage in a bout of afternoon sex with him. *Truly, she wasn't, even if she had to force herself to remember that.* She was here to tell him about his mother and she needed to focus on that. "No."

"No?" As if the conversation they were having and what their bodies were doing were two different things, he slid his leg between hers with a quick, jerky movement, forcing her thighs apart. "You want to play more mind games with me?"

The feel of his steely-muscled thigh wedged against her most intimate spot almost blew her away. Her communication skills dropped to almost nothing as she parroted his words back to him. "Mind games?"

He dropped his hand from her chin and it landed on her breast, finding and squeezing her nipple. Sensation exploded in a kaleidoscope of colors. "Mind games, you little witch. Why are you here if you're not giving up?"

Angie felt the brush of his thumb against her nipple as a damp heat flooded her panties. "I have...I have something to tell you," she managed to mumble, vaguely recognizing that there was a subject about his mother that needed discussing, but not having a clue what it was since her brain was so jumbled.

His mouth fell to her ear. "I have something to tell you, too." The rush of his hot breath against her inner ear sent shivers of delight to the pit of her stomach and his next words almost made her faint. *"I want to strip you naked and fuck you from behind."* His hands slid between them and with rapid movements, began unfastening the front enclosure of her pants. "But first I'm going to fuck you with my tongue until you scream."

He began pushing her pants down her hips almost violently, and her heart thundered, her skin prickled with the hazy memory of something he'd previously said to her. "Wait—"

He cut her off with his lips on hers, his tongue delving deep into the interior of her mouth, making gooseflesh rise on her skin as sexual need, hot and heavy, held her in its grip. She couldn't catch her breath as he stroked her tongue with his, and with both panic and arousal, Angie felt the material of her pants slide down to her knees.

Impatiently, he pulled her panties to the side, and in sync with the next stroke of his tongue, Angie felt herself impaled by a thick, blunt finger. At the impact, her body arched, and he took immediate advantage and pushed further inside. Her body held his finger snugly, and she adjusted her stance minutely, to give him more room. The back of her head hit the door as her legs weakened and her knees shook as he claimed her with his hands.

His mouth left hers and with his finger finding and stroking a sweet spot deep inside her, her eyes opened and she found him staring at her, his nostrils flaring.

Explosive currents of need raced through her, her heart hammering so strongly it almost hurt. The blood pounded in her veins and coalesced in the spot deep inside where he stroked her. Her eyes began to close again and when she heard his threatening growl, they flew open. "Don't shut me out while I make you come."

There was something in that demand that sent a strong arrow of trepidation bleeding through the pleasure Angie was feeling. Abruptly, the warning he'd given her before began blaring through her head in a series of alarm bells. She stared at him and then shook her head, "No." He *seemed* to only want sex, but all she could hear was the silken thread of caution reverberating through her memory. *It wouldn't be just fucking with you and me. If you ever made the mistake of sleeping with me, it wouldn't be just sex. So, I'm warning you now. I'd own you.*

His lips curled over his teeth in a snarl, "No, what?"

"I don't want you to make me come." As she said it, she began pushing at him, trying to get free, her brain functioning again, for the moment at least, overruling the needs of her body. It was one of the hardest things she'd ever tried to do, but she had a sudden, overwhelming need to listen to her brain and not her libido.

An enraged snarl left his throat as she sank both of her hands around his arm, trying to dislodge him from her body. He pushed against her for the space of two seconds before pulling away from the juncture of her thighs.

The immediate sexual threat was gone but before she could breathe a sigh of relief, his hands sank into her hair and held her scalp strongly, his fingers biting into her. He stared down at her with accusing, molten eyes and his words were laced with icy contempt, "Are you being a tease on purpose? Did you come here with the intention of playing a fucking game with me? Because I assure you, *I don't like it.*"

His eyes riveted her to the spot. His jaw was clenched; there was a visible tic in his cheek and he looked as if he could attack at any moment. She licked her suddenly dry lips and shook her head with a jerky movement. "It's your…your mother."

His eyes narrowed. "What about my mother?"

"I came here to tell you…" Angie sucked in a breath and tried to calm her raging heartbeat. "I came here to tell you that she came to see me."

His curt voice deepened, "When was this?"

"A few days ago. She made an appointment for next week, for me to do her hair. But she was very clear that she wants to talk about *us.*"

"Us?"

Angie nodded before she could form a reply. "You and me."

His grip lessened infinitesimally and she could see his brain ticking. "That's why you're here? In my office?"

She nodded her head again. "I don't know what you want me to say to her. I don't want to carry on with more untruths. But she's your mother and this is really your call."

He pulled back from her, removing his hands from her scalp but not moving away from her. One finger slid down her cheek before he put his forearms on either side of her head in an enclosure she couldn't escape. His expression stilled and grew somber. "Do I owe you an apology?"

The question itself sounded contrite to Angie, and her heart rate came down a notch. "I think we're okay."

"I was rough on you," he said smoothly, with no expression showing on his features, but the words themselves soothed her.

"It's all right." After a slight pause, her hands landed lightly on his hips, both because she missed the connection and to show she held no animosity.

His hand left the door and settled around her chin, lifting it gently. "I'm having a hard time staying away from you," he said, as if admitting his greatest sin.

Stunned by his honesty, Angie didn't try to contain her answer, "I'm having a hard time, too."

He stroked her bottom lip as his face grew taut. "Maybe we should do something about it."

She flushed and shook her head, keenly aware of his scrutiny. "You tripped me up with the verbal warning the other day."

His forehead fell to hers and he whispered, "It was a lame attempt to scare you away."

Her heart fluttered wildly in her chest. "I think it worked."

"Forget what I said."

At his words, the air around them electrified, but she tried to hold onto her sanity. "I don't know if I can. You seemed pretty serious at the time."

"I was pissed at my mother that day and I took it out on you."

Angie didn't know if she quite believed him but her curiosity was roused.

His hand ran up her cheekbone before sliding down to touch her lip again. A shiver ran through her but she pretended not to be affected. "So what are you saying?" she asked.

He shrugged his shoulders in a nonchalant attitude that she didn't quite believe was nonchalant at all. "We don't have to let anything get out of hand," he said in a controlled voice, but not really answering her question.

Was he trying to talk her into something, just as he'd warned he might? She swallowed hard and asked, "And by that, you mean, nothing serious has to happen between us?"

His finger continued to scrape back and forth across her bottom lip. "Nothing serious."

She felt another ripple of excitement. She didn't know if she believed him, though. "Casual?"

He looked as if the word pained him, but he agreed quickly enough. "Sure."

"What about your mother?"

He scanned her critically. "What about her?"

"We tell her the truth? That our relationship is casual?" she clarified.

A muscle flicked at his jaw. "No. The less she knows the better. As far as she's concerned, we're friends, nothing more, no relationship."

"Just friends?" she questioned.

"Just friends," he agreed.

Angie cleared her throat. "And are we?"

His hand left her face as he threaded his fingers through her hair. "What?"

Her pulse became erratic as she questioned, "Are we friends?"

His gaze became almost glazed as he glanced down at her lips and lingered there. Finally, he raised his eyes to hers, but he took his time about answering. "Sure. Why not?"

Why did she get the feeling they were at cross-purposes? "I can't…I can't think of a reason."

A half-smile twisted his lips. "As my friend, will you let me buy you dinner tonight?"

The butterflies that had been humming low in her stomach took flight and began beating against her breastbone, because she knew that dinner was definitely not the only thing on his agenda. *Say no. Say no. Say. No.* She waited a prolonged second before answering, "Okay."

A look of satisfaction crossed his face. "Then, fine. I see no reason we can't be friends."

Her doorbell went off at seven o'clock on the dot that evening. Her nerves had been shot the rest of the day, knowing he was coming to get her, and now, as she opened the door, she took a sustaining breath as she found him leaning negligently against her doorframe.

"Hi." The word was a croak from her throat.

His gaze dropped to her black stilettos and a subtle tension seemed to take hold of his body. "Hello."

"I'm ready to go."

He twisted his head to look inside her apartment, but he made no move to try to go inside. He glanced back at her and cocked his head in a motion for her to follow him. "Let's go."

Angie closed the door and locked it with fingers that shook, and as they walked down the exterior stairs, she held tightly to the rail, the heels on her shoes and the trembling of her limbs making the descent more difficult than usual.

He didn't try to rush her as he led her over to his Mercedes; he opened the door for her and stood back as she sat down. The door closed with a quiet snap, and as he was walking around the car, Angie tried to settle her nerves by taking a few deep breaths.

It didn't work; the only thing it accomplished was to make her hyperventilate.

When he opened his door, sat down and started the engine, her heart rate was still too elevated for comfort. She looked around at the interior of the elegant vehicle, at the detailed luxury, and she knew, without a doubt, that they lived on separate planets.

He looked at her but remained silent, the engine idling.

After a moment, she couldn't stand his hooded stare any longer. "What?"

He let out a sigh, and leaned over and pulled the strap over her shoulder, and buckled it into place. Her heart began pounding a loud cadence, and when he placed a simple kiss on her forehead, she about lost it—her nerves were all over the place. She was elated; she was terrified.

He didn't make idle chatter as they drove to the restaurant, and before long, they were sitting in a corner booth with a bottle of wine between them.

"You didn't wear the lipstick," he accused lightly.

She took a sip of her wine before answering, "You said it was too much."

"It *would have been* too much if I was forced to stand in a room full of other men and watch them staring at you as if you were fair game."

The smoldering fire in his eyes, combined with his silken words, made a hot ache begin to grow in her belly. "Oh."

"Oh, what?" He reached across the table and picked up her hand in both of his and began to play with her fingers.

Her heart beat unmercifully. "Okay...I know you want me to wear the lipstick."

He studied her, making no attempt to hide the fact. "I want you to wear the lipstick when it's just you and me, like it is tonight."

The blood surged from her fingertips where he caressed her. "We'll see," was the only answer she could manage.

He raised one wicked eyebrow. "We'll see?"

She shrugged a shoulder. "Casual, right?" she challenged, in a bid to remind him of their agreement, which surely didn't include him telling her what to do.

He released her hand and leaned back in his seat, picking up his wineglass.

When he only stared at her from across the table, she asked, "Right, Damian?"

After studying her for what was almost too long for comfort, he responded, "We'll see."

The way he copied her words but turned them around made her tremble, and in that moment, she admitted that she felt an unequivocal and total attraction for this man. Trying to get a grip, she wrenched herself away from his undeniable magnetism by flipping open the menu and glancing down.

There was little doubt in Damian's mind that when he died, he was going down. *Straight down.* He already knew he was doomed, and the scam he was performing on Angie was going to cement the deal. He'd almost fucked up beyond what was repairable when he'd issued that idiotic warning to her. What the hell had he been thinking? He knew the answer to that question; he'd been trying to scare her off because he knew damn good and well that he wouldn't have the willpower to stay away from her all on his own. So, he'd tried to take the power out of his hands and damn if it hadn't almost worked.

But now he was on a course to mend his fuck-up, and she was falling for it, thank God. Yeah, she was falling for it one hundred percent, and before the night was over, he'd have her in his bed and that was all he cared about. *Fuck the rest of the world.*

He didn't give a shit anymore that she wasn't right for him. His brothers could both go take a flying leap. He was going to keep her and keep her as long as he wanted. After all, how much more damn money did his family need? He didn't really need a wife, shit, he'd been doing without one for all this time, he could continue on for a while longer. He and his brothers were already rolling in dough; they had more goddamn money than they could spend in several lifetimes. So, he wasn't going to think about the business.

For once, he was going to have what he wanted. Since the day his father had died, Damian had lived and breathed the business. He'd taken on the considerable burdens, along with his brothers, and every day of his life since had been dedicated to bringing in the money and keeping his mother and the girls in comfort.

Yeah, there was no denying that he liked the cash. He received satisfaction from closing deals and seeing the money double. And there were other residuals: the women, the real estate, the respect. He admitted that he liked his life and everything about it. He didn't mind working hard, he didn't mind the travel, he didn't mind the responsibility, in fact, he relished it all.

There was only one damn thing that made him edgy. The thought of having to tie himself to a woman solely for the business. He wanted to choose his own woman. He resented the fact that he had to think of the corporation first, even when it came to something so potentially fucking detrimental to his happiness.

But he wasn't going to worry about it right now. He was giving himself permission to do as he liked for a bit, a sabbatical from the pressure of finding the right woman. Because, evidently, he wanted the wrong woman, and for a change, he was going to do something selfish.

His mind made up, he let his responsibilities go and immersed himself in the tantalizing prospect of nailing Angie to his bed.

But first, he had to get through dinner.

He watched her from across the table, the heightened color in her cheekbones giving her a heated flush that accentuated the delicate oval of her face. Her hair was shiny and healthy, hanging in lustrous curls around her shoulders. Her beauty was exotic, and it abruptly occurred to him that this was really going to happen; the fantasy that had been fucking with him for months was within touching distance.

She looked up from the menu and their glances connected; he felt an aggressive, feral need rise in his blood. He struggled to remain seated; there was a persuasive beat in his veins that begged him to pull her from the restaurant at that very moment. He knew he couldn't do that, and it was a test of his control to appear calm. He grasped the edge of the table to keep from reaching across and dragging her from her seat. His knuckles turned white with the effort.

As his attention remained focused on her, her eyes widened imperceptibly and he saw a tiny tremor in her cheek. It hit him all at once that she was somewhat agitated around him, maybe even scared, and instead of making him uneasy, he admitted that her apprehension was a powerful aphrodisiac to the predator within him. He smelled her scent; a primal urge to pursue threatened to overwhelm him. His muscles contracted as his shaft engorged and become rigid. The urge to mate rose up and took over his senses in a compulsion that he had to physically restrain.

It became a contest to see if he could continue sitting in his seat. As he sat back with a false air of indolence, he soothed the beast inside by allowing himself to touch her.

As their eyes held, he reached out, picked up her hand, and laced her fingers through his.

Chapter Five

As Damian seized her hand in an unyielding grasp, Angie knew she was quietly panicking. She could only describe the look on his face one way. *Territorial.* He was silently watching her as if he were going to pounce at any moment. He resembled a predator biding its time, and she felt like the prey that was about to be consumed.

Unable to control her instincts, her eyes broke contact with his and slid down his tightly held body.

His massive shoulders were emphasized by the casual shirt he wore, the material clinging to muscles gone taut. He didn't resemble a businessman in that moment, his look was too powerful. His air of self-confidence was almost too much; it was as if nothing could touch him. As if he held some kind of inner knowledge that told him that he'd always come out the winner.

Angie felt like the spoils in a game that he was about to win. Her heart beat loudly in her ears as she stared at her hand held captive in his. His fingers were long, the ends blunt and callused. They clamped around her hand as if his ownership was a given.

Angie sensed that he was ready to spring into action and tighten his grip if she so much as dared to breathe wrong.

She tried to conquer the involuntary reactions of her body that might give him even more power over her. She needed no handicap right now, and with dedicated effort, pasted a serene look on her features as she attempted to keep her pulse from spinning out of control. To say she found him disturbing was a gross understatement; his gaze was sharp and assessing, yet his eyes were filled with a remoteness that refused to show the savage, inner fire she absolutely knew was beating through his bloodstream.

He wanted her. That was indisputable.

There was more than an invitation in the heated depth of his eyes, there was a primitive possession, a merciless, inflexible determination that should have sent her running. But it didn't. She sat rooted to her chair, enticed by his pagan force, beguiled by his posture of authority that demanded her acquiescence.

It was powerful shit.

Her heart pulsed an erratic beat as all through dinner, he watched her with his hawk-like eyes and his intensity never let up.

They spoke of inconsequential things, and far too soon for her comfort, they'd eaten and he'd paid the bill. He hustled her out to a night gone dark, and before long they were driving down the interstate in a direction that had nothing to do with him taking her home and everything to do with his intentions toward her.

She knew where they were going.

His hand held hers over the console, his fingers playing with hers and this thumb pressing against her pulse point, making her blood pump more swiftly.

Few words were spoken between them, but Angie knew where this was headed. She wanted it; there was no denying that. How could she not?

He was handsome, rich, and compelling, and she was only human, after all. She experienced a gamut of emotions, all perplexing, but all leading to one thing. *She wanted to go to bed with him.*

And nothing would change that.

He drove to the west side of the city, where property was at a premium, and although the outcome would be the same, she realized that they weren't driving to his condominium. Before long, he was pulling into a driveway protected by a tall, wrought iron fence. He pressed a single button on the dash, and the gate began to open.

As he navigated the long drive, Angie finally found her voice. "Where are we?"

"My house."

A sudden tension filled her when she saw the size of the structure before her. "I thought you lived in a condo."

He glanced over as he pulled the car around back. "I have a condo for convenience." His eyes gleamed like black volcanic rock. "I *live* here."

He pulled into one of four bays, and as he escorted her from the garage, the automatic lights lit up the array of other vehicles parked there. Angie made out a top of the line Range Rover, a disreputable truck that looked as if it had seen better days, and a sports car, shiny and low-slung but she had no idea what it was.

The house itself was nothing less than a mansion. Bigger even than his mother's home had been, Angie had never been in a house of this size or spectrum before, and she was more intimidated than she cared to admit.

As he led her inside and she saw the scope of the rooms themselves and the way the entire house was furnished, she realized that he was far, far richer than she had imagined. *She should have gotten a clue when she found out he owned the business tower.* She swallowed hard as her steps stalled while she looked around. The rooms were picture perfect, putting a modern spin on the traditional. Angie had no idea what she was actually seeing, she'd never been exposed to a world like this before, but she recognized instantly that the walls were filled with art, not just decoration. Across the rooms, there were elegantly pared down pieces of furniture with subtle detailing, interspersed with outrageous Victoria pieces, and yet, they coexisted harmoniously.

As she hovered in frozen amazement, Damian walked back the few steps to where she stood and with a declaration of intent, swiped her wrist and began dragging her up the ornate, sweeping staircase.

A shiver of response took her breath away, and she stumbled once before quickly regaining her footing. Her stomach tied in knots from both the reality of his wealth and the heat blossoming between her thighs; she could barely get her brain to function.

She was on automatic pilot as she followed him up the stairs.

He strode down a corridor, flung a door open and led her inside what was obviously his bedroom. She saw massive furnishings and a sitting room off to the left, but that was all the time he gave her before dragging her over to the bed. He backed down until he was sitting, and spreading his thighs wide, he pulled her between them with little fanfare. Leaving no question of his purpose, he pulled his shirt over his head and sent it falling to the floor.

Feeling bereft of control, Angie gasped as she took in his jacked physique. His biceps were like iron, his chest lined with muscles so tightly laced they showed no give. The tendons of his neck were corded and displayed a pulse working heavily as the blood beat through his veins. Her world spun and careened on its axis as he sank one arm around her waist and pulled her head down with the other, until her lips were almost touching his. His eyes were still open and he paused before proceeding. "It's going to be good." His eyes reflected a harsh, almost demonic light, but his words were sensuous, as if telling her a secret that he knew to be true.

She felt a jolt to her system and with her pulse skittering alarmingly, she responded the only way she knew how, which was nothing less than the truth. "I know."

His hand locked against her spine, drawing her torso slowly, inexorably toward his. Her breasts landed against the hard planes of his chest, and a shudder that she couldn't suppress passed through her.

A tangible, magnetic bond flowed between them as his hand caressed the contours of her back. Her reaction to his touch was swift, almost violent and he watched her steadily, making no attempt to hide the fact. She was very aware of his assessment; she felt her pulse pounding from her fingertips to her toes.

His hands caressed down and locked onto her hips, his fingers biting into her flesh. She inhaled sharply at the possessive contact. Her fingers ached to run all over him, but she attempted to wait until her pounding pulse subsided somewhat and she could attain a level of control. As shivers of attraction raced through her system, she vaguely realized that his breathing was becoming affected. He pulled oxygen in and out of his lungs in a harsh rhythm, and she could see his chest lifting and falling with the effort.

His lips fell to the side of her face, and she felt the heady sensation of his kiss slide from her cheekbone to her ear. A delicious sensation arced down her spine and robbed her of any thought capacity she may have had left. Her world became sensory; all she felt was a drugging sensation as he seared a path down her neck to her shoulders.

Her hands fell to his biceps, and the hard, tactile strength under her fingertips was such a contrast to her own body that her knees weakened. She ached for his kiss on her mouth, but the ecstasy wrought by his attention elsewhere wouldn't allow her to divert him from his direction.

He brought her more tightly into the circle of his embrace by locking his legs around her, and as if knowing she couldn't escape, only then released her hips and brought his hands between them. He began releasing the buttons on her shirt, swiftly and with feverish intent. His gaze was a hundred percent focused on what lay beneath the cloth and a noticeable tic began to pulse in his cheek.

As he pushed open the panels of her blouse and the white curves of her breasts peaked through the lace of her bra, she felt the reflexive jerk of his shoulders under her palms. He breathed deeply, and pushed the shirt off her shoulders, letting it drop to the floor. His chest rose with his intake of oxygen and his voice came out in a low growl, "I'm trying like fuck to go slow." His eyes lifted to hers and Angie was hit by such a reflection of tortured impatience that it left her almost bewildered. He pulled in a deep breath and continued, "But I'm about to lose it and it's going to go fast."

His hands gripped her shoulders as he waited for an answer and Angie tried to get her short-circuited brain to function, but all she could do was nod her head.

At her agreement, his palms sank around her breasts and squeezed, his fingers unsnapping the center clasp of her bra, releasing her flesh from constraint. He began flicking his thumbs across her nipples in a twin assault, and in a last moment of sanity, Angie asked him, "You've got protection?"

His hands momentarily stilled and his eyes lifted and crashed with hers. "Birth control?"

Angie felt his penetrating stare as if he were trying to get inside her head and see all her secrets. She didn't know why she cared; maybe it had something to do with his earlier threat of ownership if she slept with him. He'd backed off that right away, but why should she tell him more than he needed to know? A ribbon of doubt at what she was doing sneaked up on her, and she tried to ignore it, but had to give him an answer. She shrugged a shoulder in response.

His eyes hardened infinitesimally. "I'm clean. You're clean, right?"

"Of course."

"Then we don't need protection. Unless you need it for birth control?"

Why did she get the feeling that his questions had little to do with any STDs that either of them might have, as opposed to him wanting to know if she was on something? She truly didn't think he was the type of guy who would push her into having unprotected sex, especially not the first time, and that meant that he wanted to know if she was already protected against pregnancy. And what exactly was the harm in telling him that she wasn't? All of this ran through her mind in a single thought as tremors of sexual heat continued to burn through her veins. Suddenly, her brain lost focus and she couldn't remember why she shouldn't give him the answer he sought. "I'm not on anything."

Satisfaction, in its purest form, blazed from his features before his face became hooded. He reached out with one hand and retrieved a condom from the top drawer of the bedside table while holding her locked to him with the other.

He put it within reach, and with no warning, his lips landed on hers, his fingers clenching around her butt, squeezing her flesh and sending butterflies through her system. His tongue thrust into her mouth, and she felt the vibration of his groan from deep within his chest.

Damp heat flooded her, and all thoughts but him fled her mind as she concentrated on the amazing way he made her feel. He turned her head and adjusted the angle to the fit he wanted, and Angie fell into his kiss with no thought for the future and with no further consideration that she might be making a huge mistake. She knew that what he made her feel had nothing to do with reason, and in that moment, she didn't really care.

She allowed herself what she desperately wanted; she let herself feel. A pulsing knot of fevered attraction settled low in her stomach as a hot ache grew in her limbs. Her arms wrapped around his neck, and she threw herself into a kiss that was making her thighs clench in an agony of need.

His kiss contained a ferocious, hungry passion and she felt a lurch of pure, physical excitement. The first touch of his lips was slow, drugging, but it quickly escalated to a firm and urgent possession. Angie felt the swipe of his tongue and then the bite of his teeth against her lips. With one hand sliding between them and settling around her breast in a grasp so strong it made her shudder, he spoke against her lips, not taking the time to lift away from her. "Fucking. *Sexy.*" He squeezed her nipple and bit her bottom lip, and a sharp, lancing arrow of sexual need slammed her with its intensity.

His kiss turned completely fierce, dominant in its aggressiveness, and she became lost under his control. But it was a heady feeling, a perfect feeling as she let him take the lead and was allowed only to feel. Her arms clung tightly around his neck, as the repeated drag of his thumb across her nipple sent arrows of fire shooting down her spine to land in a pool of heated energy between her thighs. She blossomed and felt herself become wet, and she had no control when she began undulating against him.

The hot lick of passion was explosive between them, and with her heart thundering in her ears, she shuddered as his mouth left hers and his hands slid down and began stripping the clothes from her body with ferocious intent. She let out a small sound of fevered impatience, and misinterpreting the noise, he wrapped a hand around her wrist, halting the escape he thought she might try to make, a growl of warning coming from his throat.

He'd read her completely wrong; there was no way she was trying to get away from him and his inflexibility only heightened her arousal.

"Don't try to get away from me," he bit out, as he pushed the clothes from her lower body. He immediately lifted her from her feet with a vise-like grip at her hips and twisted around until she was lying anchored to the bed as he leaned over her. He lifted slightly, pushed off his shoes and socks, and then climbed more fully onto the bed. His movements enticed her like an addiction she had no control over, and with a precision that left her breathless, he pushed his iron-hard thigh between hers and held her fast to the bed.

His hands encircled each of her wrists and lifted them over her head, checking any movement she might have tried to make. A hot, fiery stroke of need made her stomach flip as she looked up into eyes of molten gold.

Her blood pumped feverishly through her system in waves of delight. With a feeling of aching bliss, she pushed with her wrists against his unrelenting hold as he imprisoned her. Feeling no give at all, a sharp tug of excitement coiled in a river of heat that held her enthralled.

His eyes narrowed and darkened, even as his hands continued to grasp her with uncompromising strength. His knee pushed against the juncture of her thighs in forceful threat, pinning her lower body to the mattress. "Stop pushing against me," he hissed. "It won't get you anywhere." A blatantly male look of domination crossed his features as he bared his teeth. "Here's how we're going to play this. You get *one word* that will make me pull back." He studied her with masterful authority, making tremors of heat spread through her bloodstream. "Can you guess what that word is?"

She quivered in his hold as she tried to comprehend long enough to question, "Stop?"

He lifted his chin in confirmation. "That's the word. You say 'stop,' and I'll stop. But that's the only word that will work, understand me?" She nodded her head in a jerky movement and he continued, "I'm warning you, nothing else will do the trick. I'm already too fucking far gone to figure out what all the pushing against me means." He clenched his jaw. "You trying to get loose?"

Her eyes flared in denial as the thought of him letting her go sent shards of regret through her. She began shaking her head. "No."

"That's good, because I'm not letting you go." He released one wrist and he brought his hand down and fisted his fingers through her hair in a further act of primitive possession. His intense gaze was compelling as he studied her. "Remember what you have to do to stop me, babe, because it's the only out you'll get."

With that warning heating the air between them, he bent his head and kissed her. Angie felt his ravenous hunger in the press of his lips and the stroke of his tongue as it dueled with hers. His sensual aura swept over her, and she expelled shallow pants as irresistible need clenched in her stomach. He kissed her with sure, firm strokes, taking from her mouth and swallowing the air she exhaled as if he couldn't get close enough.

She felt the same. With her one free hand, she sank her fingers into the muscles of his shoulder, feeling the hard ridge of flesh under her touch. His skin felt exquisite, his scent inflamed her senses, and the way he was attacking her mouth as if he had no control where she was concerned, was sending sparks of primitive delight dancing along her nerve endings.

She felt the vibrations of a low growl begin in his throat and bleed up through his mouth and into hers. The raw, feral sound evoked a titillating shiver of response as she felt an all-consuming need to submit to the pure pleasure he induced within her.

He pulled his mouth away and stared down at her. Trying to take in some much-needed air, she looked back in fascination. Dragging his eyes away, he glanced down and Angie was very aware that the only clothing she wore was her opened bra.

She lay panting as he released her and reached down with both hands and slid the cups of her bra out of his way. Her nipples immediately beaded, whether from the cool air or his heated gaze, she didn't know.

His cheekbones became tinged with red, and with his nostrils flaring, he swiped his thumbs across the pink tips of her breasts. Electricity arced through her and lifted her spine from the bed. At her reflexive movement, his eyes lifted to hers again and held her gaze captive. He raised a hand and with a slow gentleness, lifted a lock of her hair and began swirling it, almost leisurely, through his fingers. The calm, almost placid movement wasn't anything she'd seen from him before, and it threw her off balance. Her heart beat heavily in her chest while she waited for his next move.

His erection pressed against her leg and it looked as if his restraint was costing him. Masculine fingers tightening in her hair so much that she couldn't have moved if she'd tried, he pressed a soft kiss to her lips before looking down again. "You're even prettier than I expected," he said in reverence.

He scanned her, his eyes raking boldly over her, and his voice when he spoke sounded torn from him. "You have no idea what it cost me to stay away from you for so long."

Angie didn't know what to say, and when he dropped his head to her breast and took her nipple into his mouth and began suckling her, every thought of responding flew from her brain as a multitude of colors exploded in her head.

He licked her breast, sipped at her nipple, and fastened his mouth to the tender flesh just above the tip and began sucking with a rhythm that shut down her thought process.

He released her hair and wrapped his arm around her waist and lifted her. He held her tightly in an unbreakable embrace as he moved his mouth from breast to breast, making breathing difficult and arousing her so much she began to think she might come from just his mouth on her nipples.

She began to whimper, and he let her go, and almost violently, ripped the rest of the clothes from his body. He came back to her completely naked and Angie reached for him, but he denied her by clasping his hands around her upper thighs and forcing them apart. He crawled between her legs and looked down at her most feminine spot, which was open to his gaze and unprotected.

Angie felt a million emotions at once. She almost cringed because the light was still on and she felt a sharp arrow of modesty that she couldn't control. But she also felt arousal, hot and sweet, slide down her spine at the unadorned expression of pure lust on his face. As he continued to look between her legs with a mesmerized expression, a groan rattled from his chest and exploded from his throat with such force that it shook the bed. "Need. To. Fuck. You."

At his words, a bloom of heat exploded between her thighs as a current of sexual need made the oxygen hitch in her throat.

He reached down with both hands and put his fingers on her inner lips and spread her out, while he examined her to his fill. A subtle tension shook his shoulders and holding her pressed open with one hand, he slid his long, middle finger inside. Angie cried out as sensation held her in its grip. He grunted from deep within his chest as he manipulated his finger inside of her.

Lost in a world of exquisite sensations, Angie reached down and found his hard shaft. At the first touch of her fingers, he reared back from her and pushed her hand away. "You want it over already?" he growled.

She began shaking her head back and forth on the pillow in denial, and he took his touch away from her feminine core. He lifted his hands toward hers and motioned with demand, "Hands. Now."

"What?"

"*Give me your hands.*"

With a rush of trepidation battling the primitive hunger in her veins, Angie slowly relinquished her hands to him. He sank his fingers around her wrists and planted them at either side of her hips in a grip that dominated her and gave him absolute control. Holding her immobile, he wasted no time, and dropping his head between her thighs, placed his mouth on her and began kissing her in the most intimate way possible.

Sexual need, hot and fierce slammed down her spine as he began licking her, spreading his tongue out and swiping her from top to bottom and back again. Back and forth, over and over until she was blistered with a need so profound that she wouldn't have been able to describe it if forced to.

He sank his mouth over her clit and raked his teeth across it, and the feeling was so indescribable that she saw stars. He lifted his head and with an expression etched in stone, he forced out, "I'm going to let go of your hands. *Do not* move, you understand me?"

Angie let out a tiny mewling noise.

"I mean it, Angie. You move a single inch and you'll regret it. Nod your head if you understand."

Angie nodded her head and he released her hands immediately. She fisted them into the sheet to keep them in place as his mouth dropped back down to her clit. Simultaneously, she felt his finger sink back inside of her, and with colors spinning in her head, she endured the pleasure as long as she could before she began splintering around him.

She began moaning from the back of her throat, and as he moved his finger inside of her like magic and bit into her clit just short of pain, Angie exploded in a downpour of fiery sensations.

Damian was going to lose it. He was seriously going to lose it if he couldn't get it inside of her right now. *Now.*

He withdrew his hand from her as gently as possible and reared to his knees. Gritting his teeth to keep from plunging into her bareback, he swiped the condom package from the end table and tore the plastic with his teeth. He held his straining cock in one hand, and rolled the rubber down with the other.

He moved between her thighs and pressed her open with his knees between her legs. He wanted to be able to say something to her, but speech was impossible. He felt as if he were on a tightrope; he didn't think his heart would keep beating unless he could get inside of her.

He looked down and saw that the expression of euphoria was slowing leaving her features. She glanced down and her eyes flared with a look that he could only describe as trepidation. *Son-of-a-bitch.* He knew what she was seeing. His goddamn cock was what you might call super-sized. When he'd been a kid, he'd been proud of it. But not so much anymore.

His size was nothing more than a sexual hindrance. He'd learned to choose women who looked as if they matched him physically. But there wasn't anything about Angie that matched him physically. *Nothing.* She was small and delicate and his finger inside of her had only proven that she would have a hard time accommodating him.

Studying her now, the fear he was feeling was twofold. Fear that she would bolt before he could prove to her that they *would* fit together, and for the first time since he'd been a teenager, fear that he was going to lose it before he could get his cock where it was supposed to go.

Son-of-a-fucking-bitch. She made him feel like a fucking teenager.

Unable to delay any longer, he positioned his erection at her entrance and began to push. He gritted his teeth and concentrated when all he wanted was to plunge inside. *Slowly, Rule.* He had to go slowly. *Get a grip, man.* Go. Fucking. Slow.

Through the tight bubble of silence that filled the room, all Damian could hear was his roughened breathing highlighted by her sudden gasp when he began the inexorable push inside. He felt her breath hitch and tension take hold of her where she lay under him as she became deathly still. He swallowed and groaned, her wet heat enclosing around the head of his cock, giving him a teasing glimpse of the pleasure he was about to find, if he could only get it inside.

He pushed again, trying to attain another inch of depth, but her internal muscles tightened and her hands came up against the planes of his chest in a defensive move. She didn't push against him, *thank God*, only held her hands there as if ready to call a halt. A bead of sweat formed on his forehead. She was so tight that his brain was almost spinning. A tantalizing lick of fire along his spine urged him to push again. He asserted ruthless control and reminded himself what the definition of *slow* was. He fought the predator inside and with deliberate discipline, pushed again.

He stalled instantaneously when she let out an alarmed little moan and her fingernails clenched into his skin, stabbing into him. He felt her suck in a breath and hold it, and he knew that she was silently panicking. *God, he needed time.* He needed time before she refused to go any further. With that in mind, he set out to calm her. His arms came down on either side of her head and he dropped his mouth to her ear, and took a moment to calm himself first, dragging in oxygen in a repeated attempt to slow his heart rate.

He was as hard as a rock, the blood pumping furiously through his veins, landing in an erection so hard that it was painful not to continue pushing. He fisted one hand in the sheet and the other in her hair and tried to speak while fighting his arousal. "Hey, baby, *it's okay,*" he whispered. "It's going to go in." Her whimper of denial sliced through him and he felt a pounding in his head. "Shhh, shhh," he mumbled disjointedly in an effort to soothe. "You're doing great, baby. Just keep still for another minute, okay? I promise it won't hurt if you let me be easy."

Her grip relented slightly as she lay still and listened to him as if his voice was the only anchor she had. "That's it, sweetheart. Relax. Can you relax your muscles for me?" He pressed his mouth to her ear and grazed a light kiss over her lobe. "I don't want to hurt you." He took her lobe in his teeth and pulled with a slight friction and he heard her breath catch and felt some of the tension leave her body. Relief, hot and sweet, slid down his spine. "You're *so sweet*. The last thing in the world I want to do is hurt you."

She made a tiny keening noise and Damian slid a hand between them and pressed a finger on her clit. With a control he didn't know he had, he took his time and swirled his touch over her silky flesh repeatedly until she moaned again. Another rush of relief gripped him by the throat as she arched against him and he felt a sudden rush of feminine moisture around the head of his cock.

Thanking whatever deity that might be listening to him, he lifted his hips and pushed in a short, firm stroke that only allowed him to sink another inch inside her. His guts clenched with violent need; he was at that incredible, tight threshold at the point where her body needed to give. He groaned and pulled back before pushing in again.

Her breath caught again and her fingers sank into his skin in warning.

She was tight, tighter than even he'd expected when he fantasized about her and the knowledge of that was sending a throbbing, primal beat through his system. He wanted to slam into her so badly he could taste it, but he knew he couldn't. She held herself too still, almost holding her breath, as if expecting to be hurt at any moment, and her fear wasn't sitting well with him. He redoubled his efforts and continued to play with her clit while he attempted to seduce her with words. That the words he spoke were the complete truth didn't escape him. "I've never felt anything half as good as you feel. I knew it would be good the first time I saw you." He slid over and kissed her on the lips and then rose up enough to see her face. Her eyes were closed with a look of concentration on her features. "You're so pretty, baby. You feel so good."

Through a haze of lust, he watched the expression on her face turn to mesmerized, as she lay perfectly still and listened to him. "You're doing so well, sweetheart, being so still, just like I told you to. You're a good girl, aren't you?" Unable to help himself, a barrage of emotions slamming through him, with savage possession he leaned down and softly bit her lip. She cried out, and at the same time, he felt another wave of moisture that allowed him to sink deeper inside.

Chapter Six

Damian groaned at the same time that Angie moaned, and he lifted and began stroking, pushing in a bit at a time until he was fully seated within her. Satisfaction and arousal blazing down his spinal cord, he rose up on his hands, his elbows locked in place as he studied her.

Her eyes were closed and he felt a need so strong he couldn't contain it. "Angie. Open your eyes."

She stalled for the count of two seconds, but then her eyes flew open and she looked up at him. "It's in," he announced with a triumph he couldn't hold back. "And it feels good. Fucking perfect." He slid out and took another stroke and her eyes began to slip closed.

"No," he grunted. Her eyes opened and she watched him though heavy lids. "Am I hurting you?" Without waiting for an answer, he continued with some satisfaction, "I know I'm not."

She shook her head.

Holding himself up with one arm, he slid his hand back to her clit and massaged her there, the fullness of his cock inside of her, so close to where he touched her intimately, adding another dimension to his need. "You want to come again?"

Her eyes flared but she remained quiet, and he said, "I think you want to come again."

Shaking her head, she whispered, "I don't think I can."

"No?"

She visibly swallowed, and shook her head again.

She might have doubts, but Damian had none as he felt her sweet, slick wetness surround him. He began taking firm, short strokes, and with every inward thrust, he hit that place deep inside of her that he knew would drive her crazy. Within seconds, she was moaning in the back of her throat. Within a minute her eyes closed and so did his.

The fury of sexual heat consuming them both, he let his instinctive reflexes take over. He stroked her hard and deep, taking what he needed, what he felt like he had to have to keep breathing. With a last, hard, merciless pump, he thrust them both into a world of sublime pleasure. She let out a high, feminine shriek, and holding himself tightly inside her, milking the spasms of release, he followed her over the edge into a pleasure so profound, he felt stunned.

In the aftermath he tried to clear his head, but thinking was impossible. He slid to the side, withdrawing from her as gently as he could manage, allowing her to breathe deeply. He was pulling in oxygen as if he'd just run ten miles, and before he could check the inclination, he swept her up in his arms and held her clamped to his side with one arm around her waist as he lay on his back.

A feeling of possession swamped him, one he immediately tried to tamp down. A dark, dormant emotion from deep in his soul abruptly reared its head and he felt aggression rise in his blood. Just the simple act of pulling out of her was causing conflict in his brain; he struggled against a compulsion to not let her go.

A thousand thoughts hit him from all sides. The fact that it had been the best fucking sex he'd ever had was the most prevalent, the memory sliding over him and even now, hardening him to a full-blown erection. The feel of her was like an addiction; she was soft and feminine and the fact that he wanted to stake a fucking claim was screwing with his heart but his head was fighting the desire. *Nothing* had changed and he needed to remember that. She was still wrong for him. Maybe the sex *had* been the best in his life, but sex didn't count for everything. He had to remember the other qualities that were important in a relationship. There was compatibility, friendship, and that ever-elusive quality that he always heard about but didn't quite believe in, love.

What-the-fuck-ever. It didn't really matter. Those were problems he'd have to face in the long-term, but all he had to think about now was the short-term, at least for the moment. There was no question that she felt damn good in his arms, so for now, that's where she'd stay. He abruptly remembered what he'd told her when he'd been trying to get her to sleep with him. *Nothing had to be serious.* He knew it was a mantra he needed to live by. Even as he had the thought, he questioned whether it was viable or not. *Could* they maintain a casual affair with everything staying smooth sailing? As his arm clenched tightly around her, he acknowledged that he might have a certain difficulty with that. And *why* shouldn't it be easy to keep things casual?

He didn't feel casual.

And he didn't know if it would *ever* be possible to feel only casual with Angie.

Had someone told Angie a few months ago that she'd have a hard time chatting with Damian's mother, continually reiterating to the older woman that she and Damian were only friends, she wouldn't have believed them.

But it was so true. She was having a damn hard time. It happened every time the older woman came in for a cut.

As Mrs. Rule sat in the chair at her station, Angie couldn't help a shard of discomfiture at the lie she was perpetuating. Maybe if it had only been that one night between the two of them, it might have been easier. *But it hadn't been.* Maybe if it had only been a week or two of hot and heavy. *But it hadn't been.* It had been *months*. Months and months of a hot affair where almost every night was spent together. Every night when neither one of them had a conflict, they'd ended up in bed together.

Damian had shown up at her apartment the night after their 'first date' without any warning, and within mere minutes, Angie had found herself butt-assed naked and clinging to him, more than ready for round two. A date had turned into two dates and weeks had turned into months now.

Maybe it was only casual, maybe it wasn't, but it damn sure wasn't a simple friendship as she insisted to his mother every time the older woman came into the salon. "Yes, I think he's really handsome," she answered, biting the inside of her cheek, as she applied the highlights that would give the much-needed definition to the older woman's hair. It had taken a while to convince her to allow highlights, but now the older woman loved them and seemed to trust only Angie to do them.

"Then why exactly are the two of you just friends?" Justine Rule asked for what seemed to be the hundredth time, her tone one of frustration.

Angie attempted to stifle the clang of warning in her head that was telling her nothing good could come of this conversation, as she tried to stick as close to the truth through the web of lies spilling from her mouth. "We don't have a lot in common, I suppose."

"He likes you, I can tell. The night of my dinner party, he couldn't keep his eyes from you, darling," the older woman said with a fondness toward her that made Angie feel even guiltier.

She felt a flush of crimson climb up her cheekbones. "I'm sure you're exaggerating. We don't know each other that well. Just from the salon, really."

"He must have wanted you to be with him that night. I just don't understand. Did he even give a hint he might like to see you again?"

A rock crawled up and lodged itself in her throat. Mrs. Rule seemed to have a one-track mind today and Angie couldn't distract her as she usually did. *Damn Damian for not wanting to be honest with his mother!* Answering this question would be a full-blown lie, and it was making her very uncomfortable. "No, he didn't really mention much that night. I got the idea that he only needed an escort for the evening."

"You know why, don't you?" Mrs. Rule asked conspiratorially.

"Umm—" Angie faltered.

"It's because he doesn't care for it when I don't mind my own business. But sometimes I can't help it; I love Courtney so much and want to keep her in my family. And marriage to one of my sons would do the trick. But I suppose Damian thinks of her as a sister. Anyway, he was trying to teach me a lesson, I think."

"Maybe so." Angie shrugged. *Maybe Damian did think of the girl as a sister, but it had been obvious to Angie that one of his brothers didn't.* "But he is a grown man, Mrs. Rule. I'm sure he'll find someone in his own good time."

"Well, he's taking too long! He'd be happier if he would settle down with one woman."

Angie felt a knot grow in her stomach and couldn't help asking, "Does he date a lot, then?"

"Oh, my yes, although I don't know if I'd call it 'dating.' He has a lot of women, darling, but they seem to be interchangeable, although I haven't seen him with anyone lately. That's why I think you'd be perfect for him. You're so attractive and... and," she paused as if searching for the correct word to describe Angie's style. "And vibrant!"

Angie smiled at the other woman in the mirror. "Thank you." She realized in that moment that Damian didn't understand his mother completely. He'd taken Angie to her dinner party with the belief that his mother wouldn't like her because of the way she looked, but that wasn't the case at all. The woman didn't appear to Angie to be judgmental at all, and she gave her credit for that.

As she put the cap on Mrs. Rule's head before leading her to the hair drying station, Angie glanced to the front of the store and saw her next appointment, an older gentleman who'd been her customer for a long time. She smiled across at him, knowing she'd have plenty of time to fit him in while Damian's mother was under the dryer.

At her smile, he stood up and intercepted them as she and Mrs. Rule crossed the room. "How are you, hon?" he asked Angie, his gaze skimming away from her to land on Damian's mother.

"I'm well, and you?" Angie questioned sincerely. She was fond of this man—he was a sweet old guy. Both he and his grown son had been her customers for a long time.

His eyes never wavered from Mrs. Rule and Angie was shocked to see a blush on the older woman's face. "I'd be better if you'd introduce me," he said in a gruff voice, nudging his chin toward his intended target.

Angie took a deep breath, a ribbon of both humor and panic rushing through her. Why did she have the feeling that Damian wouldn't care for his mother getting hit on? And with the look on the man's face, that was exactly what was probably going to happen. "Mrs. Rule, this is my long-time customer and good friend, Rick Harris. Mr. Harris, this is Justine Rule."

Mr. Harris picked up Mrs. Rule's hand and actually kissed it, and Angie broke into a spontaneous grin as the other woman's expression became colored in panic, her free hand flying up to her head as if only now remembering the colorant cap she wore.

Angie took pity on her and led the blushing and stuttering woman to her seat, adjusting the heat and setting the timer.

She began to turn away but stopped when trembling, feminine fingers grabbed her hand. She looked down at Justine. "He's very good-looking for an older gentlemen, isn't he?" Damian's mother asked.

Angie knew they weren't talking about Damian anymore, and she glanced over at Rick Harris and studied him a moment. He was good-looking for an old dude, something she'd always known. His son was exceptionally good-looking, as well. "Yes, he is."

"And is he?"

"Is he what?" Angie asked.

Damian's mother took another quick glance across the room before returning her attention to Angie. "A gentleman."

Angie smiled, relieved she could put the older woman at ease on that score. "Yes, he's always respectful; he's a gem, actually."

"Is he married?" Mrs. Rule asked as her gaze darted back and forth between Mr. Harris and Angie.

"No, his wife died several years ago."

"Oh."

Angie paused as she considered Damian's mother. The older woman was quite pretty and she took good care of herself. It was obvious where Damian had inherited at least some of his good looks. Studying her, Angie could plainly see the conflicting dismay and excitement the woman was feeling from being scrutinized so boldly. "What do you want me to say if he asks about you?"

"I don't...I don't—"

Angie took pity on her and patted her hand and whispered conspiratorially, "I'll figure something out if it comes up. I'll buy you some time, okay?"

"Do you think he'll ask?"

Angie glanced back and could plainly see the man staring in their direction. "Oh, yeah. He's going to ask."

Damian's mother blushed once again and with that, Angie turned to give Mr. Harris her attention.

※

That evening, after being herded into the bedroom, stripped of clothes and made love to within an inch of her life, Angie clutched the sheet to her bare breasts and peeked over at Damian. He appeared to be either falling asleep or deep in thought. Angie knew what she had to do. "Your mother really gave me the third degree today."

He pulled his arm from where it lay resting over his eyes and snagged her with his gaze. "She had *another* hair appointment today?"

She nodded, pursing her lips.

His brows came together in a frown. "How bad was she?"

"She wasn't *bad*, Damian. She's sweet, but she asked a lot of leading questions. *Again.*"

"And?"

Angie shrugged, and at the movement, his attention strayed down to her bare shoulder. Her stomach clenched with butterflies in immediate reaction. *Weren't butterflies supposed to go away after a while? When would that stop happening, exactly?* Trying to wrestle her unruly body under control, she answered, "She asked about a lot of things. She wanted me to talk about how good-looking you are, she wanted to know if we'd seen each other lately, if you seemed interested in me."

His forehead creased and a muscle flicked furiously at his jaw. It was obvious he was angry at his mother's interference, and Angie didn't want to make it worse. "She didn't mean anything by it; it's obvious she loves you very much. I held her off with the 'friends' line again, but it felt like a lie. I get that this is *casual*," she waved her hand between them, "but I had to intimate to her that we hadn't seen each other at all, and I'm not comfortable with that."

"What's the big deal? The appointment is over, even if she comes back to the salon again, you shouldn't have to see her for a month or more."

Angie shook her head. "Wrong. She's coming again next week."

"What the fuck for?"

"She said she enjoys our time together and wants to pamper herself again. Since she *doesn't like massages*," Angie repeated his mother's words to him, "She's going to come in for a deep-conditioning treatment and a style."

"Shit," he grunted through clenched teeth.

"I'm not going to keep lying to her, Damian."

"What are you going to tell her, Angie? That we're fucking like rabbits every chance we get because I can't keep my god-damn hands off you?"

A shard of pain pierced her heart. "That's not very smooth." She paused before asking, "How do you think that makes me feel?"

"What's wrong with it?" A circle of ice ringed his mouth. "It's the truth."

"Are you saying you only come here because you can't keep from it? Are you saying you don't want to see me?"

His eyes narrowed to slits as he watched her in silence.

"That's it, isn't it? You're actually trying to stay away." Angie clutched the sheet as she sat up, immediate hurt sliding through her heart. "So what's the draw exactly? The whole Goth element?" She kept her tone flat, trying not to betray her pain. "Something you've never had before that makes sex exciting again for a staid, cynical guy like you?"

His mouth thinned in displeasure. "I didn't say that."

"You didn't have to." She swung her feet to the floor. "I'm going to shower now. You can let yourself out."

He raised himself on one elbow and leaned forward, swiping his hand out with a sudden motion and encapsulating her wrist with his fingers. "You think you can dismiss me that easily, baby?" His mouth twisted, and if it was supposed to be a smile, it held no humor.

As his grasp tightened and he began to draw her to him with a firm, inexorable pull, Angie's heart rate escalated and she breathed in shallow bursts of oxygen. She refused to let him have his way in this, no matter that the mere touch of his skin against hers intoxicated her. "I don't have a problem with a casual relationship, Damian." She was assailed with a bitterness that she didn't want to feel. "I do have a problem with you hating yourself because you can't stay away from me."

He pulled her toward him until she lost balance and landed with her hands on his chest. "I didn't say that. Don't put words in my mouth."

"Whatever." She ached with an inner disappointment. How the hell had she developed feelings for him when she'd specifically warned herself not to? It was obvious that he didn't feel the same. "I'm sticky and tired. I need a shower."

"I'm not ready to leave."

"Fine. Stay." Angie sat up and pulled at her wrist that was still banded within his fingers. He narrowed his eyes in silent warning, but finally released her. She fled to the bathroom to take a shower, and hopefully, to find a modicum of peace.

Janice looked at Angie the next morning in surprise. "You want to do *what?*"

Angie rolled her eyes. "I want to go back to my natural color for a while."

"Why? I thought you relished all the tips this look is bringing you."

Angie shrugged her shoulders. "I'm not going to completely give it up." Then she thought better of it. "Or I might. But I'll do it slowly. But the black hair has to go." And then she smiled. "But not the music. Definitely, not the music."

Janice quirked a smile. "You do like your alternative rock." And then she sobered and asked, "Is this about Damian?"

"Maybe." Angie knew it was. She'd had some fun with him, but somewhere along the line, the casual aspect had taken a turn and wasn't working for her anymore. She didn't care for the direction things were going. If he wanted out, he should just leave. It wouldn't kill her. His attitude was making her feel bad, screwing with her self-esteem, and she wasn't going to let that happen.

She was starting to feel taken advantage of. Sure, she'd given in pretty quickly and maybe that was her fault. There was the old adage about 'getting the milk for free', but it wasn't just that. He didn't let her see inside of himself very often, if at all; he kept his emotions in check.

She needed to know if he liked her for the person she was, or for the persona she'd developed. Because if he didn't like her, she needed to quit seeing him. And his reaction to the change she was thinking about would be a big indication of how he really felt. She wasn't going back to a conservative look so that she'd be more suitable to what he wanted in a woman. *She wasn't.* She would never lower herself that way. This was a simple, expedient way to figure out if her normal, everyday look, the person she really was, was enough to keep him interested in her. It was as simple as that.

"So, is it about him?" Janice questioned.

"I want to see if it's me or gothic me that he likes. Is that so terrible?"

"Nope. Not at all."

"Do you think we can fit it in today? Between customers?"

"I can make time if you can, but you might have to walk around for a few hours with it stripped."

"That's not a problem. This is a salon, after all."

The door pinged as the first customer walked in and Janice tilted her head toward the man standing at the front. "Let's get started right after him."

After an extremely busy morning, when they hadn't had a moment to start on her hair, the phone rang between customers and Angie picked it up to find an extremely excited Justine Rule on the other end. "We went to dinner last night," the older woman said without preamble.

Angie was flabbergasted and pleased all at once; she knew immediately who the 'we' was. "Are you serious?"

"Yes, and we're going again tonight."

"Wow, that's cool, Mrs. Rule."

"Justine. I've repeatedly asked you to call me Justine."

"Yes, ma'am. Justine," Angie agreed, knowing there wasn't a chance in hell she'd call Damian's mother by her first name, at least not for the foreseeable future.

"I need to ask you a question, darling. I have literally no friends who I feel comfortable having this discussion with. They're all married and quite conservative. I thought about asking Courtney but that would almost be as bad as asking Erin and I just can't bring myself to do it. Besides, TMI and all that, that's what you kids call it, right?" she rattled and then continued, "Do you mind?"

"No, go ahead." Angie held the phone between her ear and shoulder while she swept the floor, sure that the question would be about clothes or shoes and what was stylish or appropriate. *How could his mother be so sweet when Damian could act like such a douche?*

The other woman paused and then plunged into it, "Anyway…he's going to want to sleep with me pretty soon, isn't he? People don't wait long for sex anymore, do they?"

Angie choked and the broom handle dropped to the floor with a cacophonous clatter as she made a grab to keep the phone from doing the same. "I'm sorry, what?"

"Oh, dear. I probably shouldn't have blurted it out like that. But I have no one else to ask and I've been somewhat worried about the situation. And it's your fault because you're so easy to talk to and you don't appear to have a judgmental bone in your body."

Angie walked to the back room and shut the door where she'd have some privacy. "It's okay. Let me think for a minute. I didn't expect this, you know?"

"Yes, of course, darling, take all the time you need."

Angie tried to steady her nerves. Could she have a conversation like this with someone of an entirely different generation? "So, I hate to be rude, but since you're asking me about sex, I'm going to ask a probing question, but only so I can get a clear picture of the situation." She took a deep breath. "How old are you? And do you know how old Rick is? I've never asked him."

"I'm fifty-four, and he's fifty-two, I found that out last night."

A feeling of mirth took Angie by surprise. "A younger man, Mrs. Rule? Bad-ass."

"Yes, well, my husband was ten years older than me, so this *is* quite different."

Angie took in a deep breath and blew it out, preparing herself to answer the question at hand. "Yeah, he's going to want to sleep with you if the relationship continues."

"That's what I thought." Angie could almost see the older woman twisting her hands together. "What do I do?"

Damian would murder her if he ever found out about this conversation. Screw Damian, he was an asshole. "Um, do you want to sleep with him?"

"Yes, between you and me, it's fairly exciting to think about. I've never slept with anyone besides my husband. I was young when we married, and after he died, I was so devastated that I never wanted anyone else, even though I was pursued a bit. He's been gone for seven years and maybe it's time. I don't want to be alone forever, I need my own life. I can see it upsets the children when I'm too clingy and nosy."

Angie tried to pretend she was talking to a regular woman and not to Damian's mother. "Well, I'm not an expert on sex and relationships. I have an aunt and uncle about your age but they've been married forever, and I seriously doubt they're having a lot of sex and if they are, I *don't* want to think about it. So I don't really know anybody who is new to dating in your age bracket but I'm sure it's done all the time. I mean, what with all the internet dating sites and all."

"I don't know why I'm so worried about this, but I just don't know how to go on." The agitation in the other woman's voice was easy to hear.

"Okay, here's the deal," Angie tried to be forthright. "I'm assuming that at your age, there's no risk for pregnancy."

"None at all."

"Okay, but you still have to use condoms, you know? It's for protection against STDs and HIV and other diseases and stuff. That's the rule."

"Oh, damn, I knew you were going to say that."

"I know that Mr. Harris *seems* like a gentleman, but I saw the way he was looking at you, and who the heck knows if he's new to dating since his wife died? I know he's been carrying a torch for her since she passed away and that was a few years ago, but that doesn't mean he hasn't been out trying to ease his pain with other women, you know?" Angie shook her head at herself, not quite believing she was having this conversation.

Only silence came across the line and Angie continued, "I'm not saying he's for sure been out messing around, but we don't know either way, so you have to make him use a condom." God, she felt like a mother preaching to her daughter. A daughter who she didn't really want to have sex, but needed to make sure she was careful if she did. *Oh, God, she was going to make a terrible mother.* And truly, Angie didn't care if Mrs. Rule was sexually active or not. Actually, she thought it would be kind of cool if she did have a real life; it was nice to think you could still be a sexual creature even after menopause. *But Damian wouldn't like it. What did she care? She'd been upset the night before and he'd cared so little that he'd promptly fallen asleep.*

"Should I have condoms on me? Just in case?" Mrs. Rule asked, somewhat breathlessly.

"Oh, dear Lord," Angie breathed out in a sigh, foreseeing a shopping trip in her future. "Are you brave enough to buy them?"

There was a heavy silence on the other end. "I'm not sure."

Angie tried to imagine being fifty-four years old and about to have sex for the first time in seven years and took pity on her.

"Okay, look. I'll go buy them tonight. Come by tomorrow and I'll have a box for you."

"Thank you so, so much, darling. I'll owe you one, okay?"

"Sure, but keep him at arm's length tonight, okay? Because you won't be prepared. We're really busy today and I can't get away, or I'd go get them now."

"That's okay, I'll be there tomorrow, and I appreciate it more than you know. I knew you'd be the perfect person to talk to about this. Now what else do I need to do when the time comes?"

"Do?" *Uh-uh. No way. She wasn't going there.* "I have no clue. You can probably just follow his lead, you know?" Angie replied, desperately ready to get off the phone.

"Okay, yes. That's what I thought. And after tonight, I'll hide a condom in my purse just in case."

"Right. Just in case," Angie agreed.

"Now darling, where do I buy really pretty underwear? I mean the really nice stuff, matching sets. Lace. You know what I mean."

Angie imagined Damian finding out she'd told his mother where to buy lingerie with a man in mind and she reached up and began rubbing her temples where a stress headache was beginning to form. Yeah, there wasn't a chance in hell that she'd be telling him about this phone conversation. Luckily, his mother spoke again before she had to. "There's a store at the mall called Victoria's Secret. I've never been inside but do you think that's the place to go?"

Angie breathed a sigh of relief, knowing she was about to get off the phone and put this uncomfortable conversation behind her. "Sure, definitely try Victoria's Secret first."

They'd been so busy at work that day that the black dye was still in Angie's hair when she walked inside her apartment that evening with a pharmacy sack in her hands. She tossed it on the small dinette table and went to take a quick shower.

She was feeling particularly edgy tonight, still upset at Damian's callousness from the night before. She didn't want to be here if and when he showed up. And she knew he would. Well, she didn't know for sure, but she figured. With that thought in mind, after she dried off and threw on jeans and a t-shirt, she picked up her phone and sent him a text. *I won't be home tonight. Catch you later.* That was easy enough, right?

Wrong. His text came back three seconds later. *Where will you be?*

Angie didn't stop to think, she just began to key in her response. *Out.*

Where?

She stiffened her spine as she focused on that one word demand and began keying again. *There's nothing casual about you asking me where I'll be.*

His response came back instantaneously. *Fuck casual.*

She sucked in a breath. To say she was floored was an understatement. And on top of that, she had no idea how to respond. Suddenly more antsy than she'd been five seconds ago, she slid on a pair of flip-flops and grabbed her bag and her keys, preparing to leave the apartment that very second.

She opened the front door and immediate trepidation slid down her spine. Damian stood in the threshold, over six feet of pure testosterone, leaning into hands that were propped on either side of her door frame, effectually imprisoning her inside the apartment.

She had a wild idea of darting under one of his arms, and before she could think better of it, she made a hasty dash for freedom.

He swooped down and caught her around her midriff and lifted her off her feet. Holding her in midair with one arm, his strength was indisputable as he walked inside her apartment and kicked the door shut behind him.

Chapter Seven

Angie's body tensed up, and when Damian sat her on her feet, she immediately began backing away from him.

It was an amateur mistake. After sleeping with him for so long, she should have known what his reaction to that move would have been. But she wasn't thinking. She was on auto-response, her limbic brain doing the thinking for her, her reflexes taking charge when her fight or flight response had gone into action.

She should have stood her ground and not been leery of having a verbal confrontation with him. That would have given him pause and she might have had a chance to win this battle that suddenly waged between them. But instead, she'd screwed up and he was already tracking her across the room.

She fucked-up even more by continuing to scoot backwards, until her spine was flush against the wall. He stopped six inches away and placed a single hand on the sheetrock above her head and leaned in as he stared her down.

"Where were you headed?" The question was asked softly, in a voice like silk but with an underlying edge of steel he couldn't hide.

She shook her head, refusing to give him an answer.

His burning scrutiny held her in place. "Where were you headed?" he asked again, his cool tone dropping by a tension-filled degree.

She licked her too-dry lips. "Out."

His eyes dropped to her lips before ensnaring her gaze again. "'Out' isn't an answer."

"It's the only one you're going to get."

Her voice wasn't belligerent, it was softly spoken, but it was obvious that he took the content of her words as a challenge. His muscles tensed and he gave her a dark, layered look of hostility. "Since you won't give me an answer, I guess that means that instead of leaving, you'd rather stay here and fight with me." His hands reached for her upper arms and held her in a punishing grip. "That means I'm more important than whatever you had planned, if in fact, you had anything planned at all."

His arrogant, condescending words sliced through her and the residual hurt she was feeling dried up as her chest began burning with anger. "Oh, *fuck you*," she said easily. *Could she kick him in the balls right now? And how hard?* Fury almost choking her, she pulled away with all her might, but he still wouldn't release her. "Let me go, Damian."

"I don't think so, baby." One hand slid to her chin and lifted. "Something's going on with you that I don't care for and I want to know what it is."

Her jaw tightened against his palm. "You want to know what it is?" she repeated, so mad she could barely speak.

He nodded his head, his thumb running over her bottom lip as his eyes lit with a heat she forced herself to ignore.

She clenched her teeth. "You're an asshole."

She could tell her words hit him where it hurt because his thumb immediately pressed against her bottom lip, holding it against her teeth. He gave her a scalding glare and accusation burned from his eyes. "Is this about last night? I thought we'd moved past that."

Moved past it? Could he really be that dense? He'd been asleep when she'd come from the shower and gone when she woke this morning; as usual, slinking out sometime in the middle of the night, like they had something to be ashamed of. She was hit with another flare of temper. "You're pretty quick, aren't you?"

His eyes turned to gleaming slits of warning. His hand left her arm and slid into her hair; he held her hostage with his hand gripping her scalp. "I don't care for your tone, sweetheart."

"What are you going to do about it?" She lifted her chin, her expression truculent.

"You're going to find out if you keep up the attitude."

Attitude? Tone? *Her attitude?* She glared at him with burning, reproachful eyes. "You don't like *my tone?* What about yours? *'I don't care for your tone,'*" she mimicked him. "Aren't you trying to scare me into thinking you're going to hurt me or something?"

He looked thunderstruck. "Fuck, no."

"Well, you're obviously threatening me with something—"

Her words were cut off as with a look of pure frustration, his head lowered and his mouth swooped down over hers. He didn't wait for permission; his tongue plunged inside in the semblance of the sex act. He impaled her before thrusting in and out, in a fierce rhythm that pounded her body against the wall. He reached down and encircled her waist with one arm to stabilize her, while he continued to grip her skull with his other hand.

He kissed her repeatedly, a low, guttural groan emerging from his chest as he pushed against her, his erection hard and throbbing against the softer skin of her stomach. The second that Angie began sinking under his erotic spell, she began to fight it. *She couldn't be this easy.* She wouldn't be.

In that moment, like a bolt of lightning, she acknowledged to herself that she wanted *to win.* Douche or not, she liked him, she liked him a lot. Maybe not as in 'marriage-liked', but she needed time to figure out how she felt about him. And if she kept letting him have his way with everything, she'd bore him to tears within another few weeks. She was semi-surprised that he was still this hot and heavy for her. Still, she didn't like where her thoughts were going because she didn't want to play games with him. *But how the hell were you supposed to win if you refused to play the stupid game in the first place?*

With that thought, she pulled her mouth from his and twisted her head away. She began to push her hands between them. A punishing sound of protest came from his throat as he pushed his torso against her, pinning her to the wall. His fists dropped between them and pushed her hands away. With quick, methodical movements, he began unfastening the zipper on her jeans.

A streak of panic ran down her spine. Lifting her hands back to his chest, she began pushing against him but it was pointless, he was like an immovable object against her puny efforts as he continued to work on her clothing. With a last ditch effort to save her dignity before she caved and fell back in with him, she employed the word she'd yet to use in their relationship. *"Stop."*

His hands fell still between them, and he was motionless for a moment. And then he lifted his head and stared into her eyes.

"Stop," she whispered this time.

A look of tortured pain crossed his features and he began taking in huge gulps of oxygen. Finally, he released her and then slowly stepped away. He turned around and walked across the room, and then he leaned his hands against her dinette table and hung his head, breathing deeply, tension in every line of his body.

As she looked as his rigid back, she realized that this was the most emotion he'd ever shown her. His posture seemed almost vulnerable, and he wasn't storming out as she'd half-expected that he would. Feeling a sharp need to say something to make it better between them, she cleared her throat and offered him a small olive branch. "I was just going out shopping for a while."

He heard her words. She knew he did because his chest inflated with a deep breath and he stood to his full height. He didn't turn around, he just stood staring down at the table as he asked, "Why didn't you just tell me that? Why didn't you just say so? Why'd you put crazy-shit in my head? What's the big fucking deal?"

His back was rigid, and Angie was held motionless, not knowing what to say that wouldn't expose her feelings. It was way too soon and she was too confused to know exactly what she was feeling, anyway. And what kind of crazy shit had he been thinking? *Was he jealous?*

When she didn't respond, he ran one hand through his hair and swiped up a sack from her table and turned around. Her nerves took a jolt. Her apartment was always immaculate, and the bag out of place was a discrepancy that had undoubtedly caught his eye. "You've already been shopping," he accused, and Angie felt her breath congeal as she thought of what was in the bag. *It would be so much easier if he didn't open it.* Could she get that lucky?

She felt the blood drain from her face *and son-of-a-bitch*, she couldn't stop herself as she looked down at the bag before lifting her eyes to his. Panic was probably written all over her face. It was more than obvious he noticed her damning reaction.

His jaw clenched, his muscles stiffened, and his mouth shot into an unpleasant twist. Dread settling in her stomach, even though she was guilty of nothing, she felt her legs tremble beneath her as he looked down at the bag in his hand and paused. She had one second to try to stop him, and she stepped forward, preparing to swipe the sack from his hands.

But she was too late. He pulled back and upended the bag, the contents, a single rectangular box of condoms, dropping to the carpeted floor. His gaze stayed on the ground for a few seconds too long, as if trying to compute what he was seeing, and then he kicked the box across the room and stared at her with seething accusation.

She had no idea what his reaction would be, but it wasn't the one she anticipated. She thought he'd yell and rage and threaten or possibly, worse. And she was immensely relieved when he did none of those things. But still, sheer horror bled down her spine as he watched her as if he'd just found out that she'd committed a double-murder in cold blood.

And then he simply turned away and stormed across the room, obviously about to walk out of both the door and her life, forever.

Angie panicked. "They're not mine," she screamed at him.

He halted in his tracks and then slowly turned. The look on his face told its own story; he didn't believe her for a second. "Bullshit."

She shook her head. "They're not."

Scalding fury dripped from his eyes. *"You fucking somebody else?"*

Her breath hitched. "No."

"You expect me to believe that? You've been on the pill for what, a couple of months now? We don't use 'em anymore. *Why the fuck would you need condoms?"*

The expression on his face was malevolent and it sent a chill through her bloodstream. But she admitted, the box of condoms looked suspicious. Abruptly, she knew she had two choices. She could lose him, or she could tell him the truth. What good would covering for his mother do? The woman was an adult and could do as she pleased. She certainly shouldn't have to answer to her son. If Angie continued to be evasive, nothing good could come from it. He wouldn't believe her, he'd think she was lying, which she was, and there were only two possible outcomes. Either he'd walk out the door and she'd never see him again, or their relationship would become contentious. Horribly so.

She didn't think she could face either outcome right now. She didn't want to lose him this soon; she wasn't ready. She could feel her palms sweating as she made the only mature decision possible. "I can explain, but…you're not going to like it."

At the tremor in her voice, he asked again, "Are you fucking someone else?" She shook her head, violently, back and forth. "You planning on fucking someone else?" When she shook her head again, his set features relaxed somewhat, but only minutely.

He walked more fully into the room, leaned back against the table, and crossed his arms over his chest. "Explain."

"They're not mine. I mean…I bought them for someone else."

He raised one eyebrow in obvious disbelief, dipped his head, and waited for her to go on.

Her words stalled in her throat as she thought about how pissed he was going to be. Sure, his anger would change, it wouldn't be directed at her in such a catastrophic way, but he'd still be pissed. When she didn't answer, he said, "You expect me to believe that someone in this day and age is embarrassed to buy condoms? Do you have a fifteen year old brother you haven't told me about?" He snarled sarcastically.

"Damian," she tried to soothe. "They're just condoms. It's not a big deal."

"I want a name. I want you to try to convince me you're telling me the truth," he snapped, all patience gone.

She sucked in a breath. "They're for your mother."

His expression turned to one of a boxer in a ring who'd just had his bell rung. He actually shook his head, as if trying to clear it. *"What?"*

Instead of answering his question, Angie shook her head and told him how she was feeling. "I feel like I just left your mother out to dry." She took a deep breath. "Like I just threw her under the bus."

"*My mother?*"

Angie shrugged. "I'm pretty sure that you weren't supposed to find out."

"This is bullshit. You're making it up. You know damn good and well I can't corroborate your story." He turned away before zeroing in on her once again. "*My mother.* You really want to go with that?"

He continued to watch her for a few seconds with a withering stare while Angie remained quiet.

His expression changed to one of indecision, and Angie could tell that he was actually pondering whether it could be true or not. She didn't want to push the truth on him, but it *was* the truth. "I get that she's your mother, but she's a grown woman. Your father has been dead for seven years, and she's finally ready to move on. She's still vital, still vibrant—"

"Holy *fuck*," he hissed in amazement, "You're telling the truth."

Angie took a deep breath and nodded her head.

"My mother is having sex with somebody?"

Angie relaxed a tiny bit and her lips quirked. "Well, not quite yet, but—"

She stopped speaking when he held up his hand with an abrupt movement. "Don't say anymore. I don't want to know."

Her small grin turned into a smile. "I get what you're saying. But think about me! I had to have a sex talk with her!"

"*Stop!*" His eyes narrowed as he held up a hand. "Not another word. I don't want to know about it. I don't even want to *think* about it."

Angie nodded, thankful his fury had abated. She still felt some unease about the way he'd acted and the things he'd said the night before, but she had to cross one bridge at a time.

They watched each other in silence for a few seconds. "You still want to get out for a while?" he asked. "This has fucked me up. I need a drink. Have you eaten?"

"I could use a drink," she offered.

"Let's go."

An hour later, they'd eaten and were finishing up. As they waited for the bill to arrive, Damian reached over and picked up her hand. He'd had only one drink with his meal, but still, the alcohol had mellowed him just a bit and Angie could feel the heat of his palm searing into hers as he laced their fingers together. His mouth tightened as he watched her and his voice rumbled across the table, "Seeing those condoms fall from that bag almost decimated me."

His words were so low and contained such an edge of vulnerability that Angie felt a trace of tempting heat. A vulnerable Damian was new. It made her forget about his callous attitude from the night before. And it was making her heart beat more quickly. "I'm sorry," she offered, not knowing exactly what to say.

His thumb dragged back and forth across her skin. "I'm just saying, I didn't like the feeling—the thought of you in bed with another man."

"You don't have to worry about that," she whispered.

His eyes glinted and refused to release her from their hold. "Are you sure?"

She dipped her head. "Yes."

"Is it something you worry about, too?" His brows drew together with a frown. "I mean, do you think I'm still screwing other women, or do you even care?"

Her pulse went into overdrive. "Of course I care. But I know you're not. I know you wouldn't do that. I'd thought we'd agreed on that when I got on the pill."

He shook his head. "We tiptoed around the subject. Maybe we need to say it out loud. Maybe I want to hear you say loud and clear that it's just you and me." He examined her closely, his gaze focused. "Because that's the way I feel. I haven't looked at another woman since you. I haven't wanted to."

She smiled at that. "You haven't had time. It's been pretty steady almost every night, you know?"

Heat lit his eyes at the reminder and his fingers tightened over hers. "I know. And I'd like to keep it that way. I'd like you to tell me that it's just you and me. I want to hear it."

She ran her fingers over his hand. "It's just you and me."

His expression didn't change, but he began nodding his head, as if it were something he'd already known, but now had the verification that pleased him. His voice deepened as he spoke, "I want you to know, as long as we're together, you don't have to worry about anything. I'll take care of you…anything you need. Anything you want." She swallowed and nodded her head, and tried not to think about what it would be like if they weren't together. Her eyes remained glued to his as he continued, "There are only two things I want from you…two things I need really." Her pulse pounded as she waited with bated breath for him to go on. "Nobody else touches you…and I want your total compliance in bed."

At his words, the breath slipped from her lungs in a dizzy rush. "I thought…I thought I'd already given you that."

His eyes held hers prisoner. "Maybe—maybe not. From this moment going forward, I want your complete surrender, I want certain rights over your body."

Angie felt a jolt of hysteria at what he might be implying. She attempted to swallow her alarm and asked, "Are you talking about hurting me in the name of pleasure?"

His eyes narrowed into slits and he immediately began shaking his head. "Absolutely not."

Even with his denial, the blood continued to pound through her veins in sheer freight. "Are you sure? I can't do that."

He shook his head more vigorously this time. "There's absolutely nothing inside of me that wants to hurt you. The image of you feeling any kind of pain, but particularly at my hands, horrifies me. It doesn't get me off at all. If it's any comfort, you can take that to the bank."

She felt a ribbon of relief, but was still confused. "I don't understand what you're asking me for that you're not already getting."

"I want you to do what I say, Angie. In bed…that's what I'm talking about. When we're in bed together, I want you to relinquish control to me. I want your total acquiescence."

"Are you saying…are you saying that you don't want to have to stop if I tell you to stop?"

Tension lit his features as he chewed into his bottom lip until the blood was gone and it showed white. "That's not what I'm saying. I'll always stop if you ask me to."

She shook her head slowly, in confusion. "I'm not getting it."

He picked up her other hand and spread his fingers through hers, until both of their palms were touching. "I don't know how to explain this to you, because I've never felt a need like this before I met you. This isn't something I've ever wanted with another woman." A primal look of heat infiltrated the lines of his face as he attempted an explanation. "I'll always stop if you tell me to. What I'm saying is that I don't want you to tell me to stop."

Angie felt her stomach plummet and let her hands go limp. The only thing holding them up were his fingers, entwined with hers. "But that's my only out."

He nodded his head. "And you'll still have it. But I want you to use it sparingly, baby, understand?" A raw sizzle filled the air between them, a pagan, primal life force that felt tangible. "I've struggled with this, Angie, since the first time I saw you."

"What do you mean?"

"Remember what I said to you, what I warned you about?"

Her brain was more than muddled, but she thought back to that day and tried to remember his exact warning but the agitation she was feeling was too strong. "I remember you warned me about sleeping with you."

"What I said to you that day was the truth. But then I lied and coerced you into bed with me anyway." His fingers tightened on hers. "I want to own you, Angie. I want to own each and every one of your orgasms. I want you to be mine, to do with what I will. I don't want to ask for permission, I don't want to worry about refusal. From the first moment I saw you, I've felt an urge I can barely control to sink my hands around you and know that I can do anything I want to you, and nothing and nobody can stop me. Maybe that's wrong, I don't fucking know. I've never experienced the feeling before in my life."

"I don't…know what to say."

He continued as if she hadn't spoken, "I'd never physically hurt you, at least, not that I could help. That's not what this is about," he reiterated. He dropped one of her hands and seized her wrist in a grip she knew she couldn't break unless he allowed it. "You intoxicate me. Your scent drives me crazy. I feel a driving need to take everything good and precious about you and lock you in my bedroom and fuck you blind. I want to take everything that's pure and wholesome that you hide behind your gothic mask and force it out so I can touch it. Control it. I want to control you."

"You're scaring me."

He reared back from the table, a look of unease crossing his features but he didn't release her. "Maybe I need to shut up."

"Maybe you should," she said in total seriousness.

Silence pulsed between them, the soft hum of restaurant noise in the background. They sat like that for a few moments, his thumb on her wrist pressing against a pulse point she knew was racing uncontrollably. Finally, he spoke. "Say it again."

Her tongue raced across dry lips. "Say what?"

"Tell me you only sleep with me," he demanded.

"I only sleep with you," she repeated quietly.

He nodded as his features hardened. "And now say you're mine."

Angie knew what he was asking. He was asking her to agree with everything he'd just laid out about their ongoing relationship. How different could it be from what she already had with him? If he didn't want to hurt her, and she believed him on that, totally, then how different would going to bed with him be? She didn't think it would be any different, this was just some kind of mind game that was tripping him up. He was already supremely, completely dominant in bed and she allowed it, because she loved it. There wasn't a thing about going to bed with him that she didn't love already. So this just had to be some kind of a formality for him. At least she told herself as much. "I'm yours," she said in a rush before she could chicken out. Heat saturated her senses when she heard her own words.

A look of total satisfaction crossed his harsh features. "That's it then."

He paid the bill and walked her out to the car with a new sense of urgency, his hand at the small of her back.

※

Damian led Angie inside his house, the same fantasy that always fucked with his brain screaming at him now. It was a simple thing, really. They'd had sex more times than he could count, in more positions than he could remember, but he'd always held off on the one thing that made him salivate with lust.

He wanted to hold her prisoner underneath him and take her from behind. *He wanted her on all fours.*

He'd *always* wanted her on all fours, and the only reason he'd held off was because of their disparate sizes and her seeming innocence where sex was concerned.

It was obvious she hadn't been a virgin. That wasn't it. But she sometimes wore an expression of disconcertedness. Some of the things he did to her seemed to catch her off guard. Her eyes would widen, she'd wear a shaken-look, and he couldn't fail to see her body tremble.

He'd gone easy on her, at least in his own mind.

But now they'd gotten some things ironed out between them, and the new knowledge that she was exclusively his, had in fact readily agreed to that, was now sending a primal beat through his bloodstream that he couldn't ignore.

He needed to nail her to the bed, flip her over, pull her to her knees, and plunge inside.

He needed that like he needed air to breathe.

As he clamped his fingers around her wrist, her demeanor was a bit more submissive and silent than usual as he led her to his bedroom. It should have calmed him down, but it didn't. It had just the opposite effect. He felt his abdominal muscles lace with tension, the skin on his face stretched tautly across his cheekbones, and his erection was engorged to such a degree that he felt as if he might erupt from the first stroke of his fingers across her clit.

The thought sent another rush of blood to his cock. *Yeah, fuck yeah, he needed her clit.* His nostrils flared as he pushed the door to the bedroom shut and maneuvered her against it. His brain was about to explode with anticipated pleasure. He had one thought banging around in his head. *He didn't have to be so fucking careful anymore. It would be okay if she knew how insane he was about her. She wasn't going to run.*

His hands slid to her t-shirt and he pulled it over her head in a rapid movement and tossed it aside. He latched onto the pale contours of her breasts with hot eyes and watched the rapid inhalations of the breath coming in and out of her lungs as she pressed back against the door. At the sight of the pale white skin above her bra, his lust inched up a notch. "Mine," he hissed out uncontrollably, his finger running over the pale swells. "New rules. Let's give them a try," he didn't wait for an answer. He sank his fist into the center of her bra and pulled it down until her nipples popped up over the material.

Chapter Eight

Damian let out a groan that he didn't try to control and pulled down harder until Angie's small white breasts were pushed up over the material and her bra held tight below them, binding her within the twisted fabric. A raw arrow of lust shot through his veins at the sight. He pressed his thumbs over her nipples, pressing them into her body until she let out a gasp, and then he eased up and began swiping them repeatedly. Back and forth, over and over until he and Angie were panting together and he began to feel like he was foaming at the mouth.

Fire smoldered down his spine and he felt an immediate urge to take her clit between his teeth. But he refused to let go of her nipples. Her eyes were closed, her head against the door as she stood still in his embrace, breathing so hard he didn't know how she couldn't be hyperventilating. "Open your eyes."

She let out a soft moan but her eyes remained closed, though her forehead furrowed with concentration. "Angie," he growled, "Open your eyes. *Now.*"

She stiffened just a little, but her eyes flew open immediately and clashed with his. She looked completely shell-shocked, and he had a fleeting moment when he thought he wouldn't be able to wait to sink inside of her; Angie on her hands and knees might have to come later. He squeezed a nipple with one hand, while with the other, he threaded her hair through his fingers and lifted her face to his and stared down at her. "I want you to take your jeans off." Her eyes were glazed with passion as she blinked up at him. "Do it now. *Right now.*"

She hesitated, her eyes wide.

"*Angie,*" he rasped in warning.

Clumsily, but immediately, her hands fell between them and she began fumbling with the button on her jeans.

A heady sense of territorial possession filled him. If he'd been a lion, he wouldn't have been able to contain his roar of triumph.

Angie let out a shallow pant, trying to get enough oxygen into her veins to keep her brain working. It was damn near impossible. She'd never been so turned on in her life. The tight leash of control Damian always kept on his emotions was gone, blown away like dust in the wind.

In its place was an uncompromising force that held her captivated.

Her shaking, useless fingers struggled with the button on her jeans until with a low sound of impatience, he dropped to his knees and knocked her hands out of the way. The button gave and the zipper was released and his hands landed on her hips and pushed the jeans and underwear down her legs. He lifted each leg in turn, forced the material down and off until she leaned against the door in nothing but her tangled bra.

His lifted one of her legs and hooked it over his shoulder and Angie's thoughts scattered as she felt herself exposed to him. A wave of fire spread over her and a wet heat pulsed between her thighs, softening her.

He spread the lips of her sex out and stroked her with his tongue, up and down, and again, up and down. Fire licked down her spine and a moan came from her lips. His thumb reached up and rubbed over her clit, exposing it to his hungry mouth, and his teeth bit into her, just short of pain. She caught her breath as incendiary heat flowed from her head to her toes and back again.

A rumble came from his chest as he held her open, as wide as she could possibly go, and he flattened his tongue against her, scraping it up and down, over and over until she thought she'd combust right then and there.

He released her for a moment to hiss, "Give me your hands."

Swallowing hard, obeying him without a question, she reached down and he took her hands, where he placed them on the lips of her sex. "Hold yourself open. Just like that."

A stunning arrow of arousal coalesced in the pit of her stomach from the sound of his growling demand and the position he put her in. She spread herself wide and felt the moisture from her body as it dripped down her thigh.

He reached up and cupped her breasts in the palms of his hands while she held herself open to his mouth. He rasped his tongue up and down, three, four, five times, and then took her clit between his teeth. At the same moment she felt his teeth on her clit, his thumbs rasped simultaneously across her nipples.

A blaze of fire stiffened her spine and she let out an uncontrollable whimper of need. *She needed to come.* She rocked against his mouth, the twin feelings of his fingers squeezing her nipples and the sucking motion on her clit was almost too much to bear. She moaned again and without thinking, she released herself with one hand and sank her fingers into his hair.

His mouth lifted from her and he rasped out, *"Angie."*

She sucked in a breath and pulled her hand away from his hair and put it back where he demanded.

He rewarded her instantaneously with the rasp of his tongue up and down, swirling over her in a dedicated motion. She cried out, knowing she was close, and when he released one breast and brought his hand between her legs, she took a quick intake of breath.

His finger stalled at her opening and he lifted his mouth from her. "Look at me."

Angie opened her eyes and looked down and the erotic picture he made kneeling between her thighs almost did her in. She hung on a precipice as she watched him. "Don't take your eyes off me, understand?" His nostrils flared and she nodded her head in a quick little motion.

He took his finger away from her just long enough to bring it to his mouth, and with his eyes on hers, he stuck it inside his mouth, all the way to his knuckle and then brought it back out again, now glistening with warm moisture.

Her stomach clenching, waves of anticipation rushing through her, he brought it between her thighs again, ready to impale her. He squeezed her nipple in a repeated motion while she stared down at him, and as her eyes glazed, he mumbled in a roughened tone, "Make you come, baby. Want you to feel it before I fuck you."

His inflammatory words rushing through her, her eyes closed reflexively, and within seconds, much to her delight, his finger plunged inside and his teeth captured her clit and began scraping against her.

The quakes moving through her body intensified, a coil held her muscles in a tightened grip and she tingled from head to foot. His mouth lapping at her, his finger stroking in and out, and his fingers pinching her nipple with the exact, perfect pressure she needed, she exploded under his hands, waves of heat vibrating around her. Held in a fierce grip by the erotic rhythm of the powerful orgasm, it was many seconds before Angie opened her eyes and looked down.

What she saw almost unbuckled her knees. If she hadn't had the door at her back to stabilize her, she would have fallen to the ground at his feet. Damian sat on his haunches between her thighs, his mouth glistening from her juices, a feral expression stamped on his face. He released her from his intimate hold while she tried to catch her breath, but before she could, he came to his full height and swept her up into his arms.

With an arm under her back and one under her legs, he carried her over to the bed and dumped her there. As he kept his eyes trained on her without moving, he stripped himself of all clothes with harsh, economical movements. Looking back at her, he asked in a primitive, guttural voice, "Did you like that?"

Catching her breath, she could only nod her head as excitement began to build, once again, in the pit of her stomach.

As he placed a knee on the bed, he said, "That's good, baby. That's real good, because now it's my turn."

As a seductive sizzle flowed between them, Angie noticed a small difference in his demeanor and words. His motions weren't as smooth as they usually were, and he left out one small word from his sentence. The word 'okay' was missing at the end, two little syllables that would have made the sentence a question.

He wasn't asking her, he was telling her.

Before she could think much about it, her thoughts scattered as he crawled on top of her on all fours. She was flat on her back and he paused as he came over her, his knees on either side of her hips and his palms pressed flat into the mattress on either side of her head.

His gaze clung to hers, his nostrils flaring. The look in his eyes was territorial, possessive, aggressive.

He looked down and with rapid movements, he released her bra and tossed it away. A slight frown furrowed between his brows as he studied her breasts. A single finger ran over the pale swells. "Did I hurt you?"

Angie glanced down and saw his attention focused on the red lines where the elastic of her bra had bitten into her skin and left an angry mark. She hadn't even realized it was there; she'd certainly never felt any pain. "No."

His palms fell back on either side of her head and with a movement that brought his muscles into sudden prominence, he bent down and ran his tongue over the imperfection on her breast, as if to soothe her, or to make it go away. Angie was pierced with a raw arrow of pleasure. Not sexual pleasure, the emotions running through her veins were more complicated than that. She was feeling emotional pleasure from his concern.

He ran his lips up her neck and fastened them to her mouth, and he gave her a soul-destroying kiss that made her begin to question her sanity where he was concerned.

With each stroke of his tongue against hers, Angie was hit with a tingle in her stomach and a jolt to her heart. As she clung to his shoulders, arousal followed soon after. Her thighs began to tremble again and a new rush of moisture softened her.

He pulled his mouth from hers, opened his eyes and stared down at her, dragging oxygen into his lungs. As she watched him in return, her heart beat an unsteady pulse in her chest and in the secret place between her thighs.

As her blood pounded through her veins in an erratic rhythm, his features took on a dark, almost primal cast. Trying to assimilate the emotions showing on his face, she was caught unawares as his hand swooped underneath her back and he reared back on his haunches. He flipped her with only one strong arm, and she found herself face down on the mattress. Before she could get her brain functioning again, he pulled up into a position that put her on her hands and knees, his arm still wrapped around her midriff.

His hard, naked body was pressed against her back, his erection pressing into the cheeks of her buttocks. A river of unbelievable sexual heat slammed through her at the position she found herself in. She sucked in a breath and blew it out again before continuing a rhythm of breathing that was sporadic at best.

His arm felt like a vise around her waist and he leaned over her, his mouth close to her ear. He was dragging in oxygen just as harshly as she was, and unmitigated pleasure held her in its grip while she waited for his next move.

He didn't speak; she didn't think he *could* speak, he only breathed harshly next to her ear. His hand underneath her gripped her tightly and then moved to her breast and he pinched her nipple between his thumb and finger.

She cried out and he did it again. He pushed against her, his torso moving against hers in a parody of sex, and then his fingers left her nipple and slid down to her clit. He opened the fold that protected it, and then began manipulating it with his fingers, all the while breathing more harshly, the oxygen rattling in and out of his chest.

His mouth opened over the back of her shoulder and he trailed wet kisses up until he came to the place where the curve of her neck began. He licked it once, and then his teeth opened and he bit into her flesh, much as a stallion would a mare during mating. Angie let out a high-pitched sound as lightning speared through her. She began pressing her butt up toward him, unable to control the movement.

He groaned from deep in his chest and released both her clit and her neck. He reared up, and his hands landed on her hips and restrained her within his grasp.

Angie felt pressure, a huge pressure, pushing against her opening. She was ready for it. She was beyond excited, she was primed and waiting, her breath suspended as the expectation of pleasure danced through her head.

Damian tried with everything inside of him, not to slam into Angie. His abdominals were held in a tight configuration, his cock ready and poised to impale her. He took a breath, and pulled her by the hips until she was exactly where he needed her to be.

He pressed the head of his cock to the hot, inviting wetness between her thighs and swirled it around until every thought flew from his brain. He was driven by instinct, by the need to mate, by the need to pummel her until he exploded and his seed spread out and soaked her on the inside.

Fuck, he needed that shit now.

He took the mind-numbing pleasure he needed and sank his erection inside of her with one long, steady stroke until he bottomed out, hitting her womb and sending vibrations of pleasure down his spine that gripped him by the balls.

A harsh gravelly noise exploded inside the room and he knew it came from him. He was close to losing all control and he didn't think he cared.

He heard her moan blend with his groan, he felt her moisture all around him, and he began to stroke her body, in and out, until what little thought process he had left separated from his body and he became a purely physical animal.

With pleasure and need enticing him, egging him on, he pummeled her from behind, his rod thick and hard. Not far from orgasm, an uncontrollable, possessive streak grabbed him by the heart and his fingers sank deeper into her skin.

Unable to stop himself, he lifted her off her knees until the only thing holding her in a constant position were her hands on the mattress and his cock, nailed inside of her.

She began to let out a long, continuous wail, and at the sound of her impending release, he lost it completely. He began hammering at her harder, over and over, harder and harder, slamming into her until his world exploded in pieces around him.

As orgasm held him in its grip, he held himself still inside of her, as deeply as he could go, and let the peace and bliss that was Angie slide through his system and permeate his veins.

Finally, his heartbeat stilled. He knew she'd found her release as well, and he slid to his side, pulling her against him but refusing to extricate himself from her body.

Not yet. He needed this feeling for a moment more; he needed to stay inside of her for just a few seconds longer. Surely that was all he'd need before he started feeling normal again.

Three days later, when Angie opened her front door to Damian, her hair was back to its normal color, a dirty blonde.

She'd decided to go for the full shock factor, and instead of being covered in black from head to toe, since it was hot and summer was approaching, she was dressed in white, capri-length jeans and a pink, short-sleeve top.

She wore silver jewelry, subdued-to-little make-up, and her fingernails and toes were painted an oyster-shell pink.

Nobody on the street would have recognized her as the same girl she'd been twenty-four hours before.

As she opened the door and stood back with a small smile, the facade of calmness she presented to him was matter-of-fact, but on the inside, she was quaking.

What would he think? She knew she was only pleasantly pretty; there certainly wasn't anything to write home about when it came to her looks. She had an okay body, mostly because she worked hard at it, doing at least forty-five minutes of exercise, following along with the television work-out shows she favored, at least four or five times a week.

But with her make-up understated, this was the real Angie. The person she'd been until the ruse she began about a year before, and the person she'd always intending becoming again.

Of course, he'd seen her without make-up many times, she usually showered after sex, with or without him, so her face itself wouldn't come as a surprise to him. But combined with the dark blonde of her hair, who knew how he'd react? When the bad-girl image disappeared, would his interest take a dive as well?

As she held the door open, the first thing she saw was a swift show of pleasure on his features when his eyes met hers. Angie knew the look was simply from seeing her again, and she couldn't help but feel a trickle of delight when she realized he couldn't contain his feelings for her, whatever they were.

But then he frowned as his eyes ran up and down her length. His body stiffened as if he'd just taken a direct hit. She didn't have time to feel disappointment, though, because he took an immediate step forward and invaded her personal space.

One arm wrapped around her waist and with the other hand, he tipped up her chin. He smiled as if he couldn't help himself, and his eyes ran over her again and then settled on her hair for a moment before his eyes fastened to hers once again. "What's all this?" he asked in a darkly intoxicating voice.

With her heart beating loudly in her ears, Angie took a deep breath and shrugged. "Me."

He frowned as if confused and pleased at the same time, and he shook his head. "No it's not."

She studied him for his reactions. "Yeah, it really is."

Pushing her back to arms length, he spun her around, looking her over as if inspecting every inch of her. When she was facing him again, he lifted one eyebrow and questioned, "Blonde?"

"Dark blonde," she answered, "mousy-brown, really."

He let out a harsh laugh as his eyes continued to gleam. "There's nothing mousy about you."

"No?" she challenged.

He shook his head while his fingers trailed up and sifted through her hair. "This is real? This is really your color?"

"You didn't think it was jet-black, did you?"

"No, I knew it wasn't. Not with your pale skin tone."

When he didn't say anything else, she crossed her arms defensively. "What do you think?"

His hot eyes glowed into hers. "Initially, I'd say I like it." He tipped his head as if debating it and then reached down and snagged her wrist with his hand. "But I need something a little more definitive to go on."

With that, he turned and locked the door and pulled her toward the bedroom, his purpose impossible to miss.

※

Several more weeks slid by and Angie was getting in deep. She was getting in more than deep, she was falling in love hook, line and sinker.

Damn.

What to do...*what to do?*

Her changed appearance hadn't even been a blip on Damian's radar. He treated her no differently. He looked at her the same way; he made love to her the same way.

So now she knew; it wasn't the dark look that he seemed to crave. *It was her.*

And it made her happy, it really did.

But suddenly their torrid, casual *friendship* had turned into a blistering, serious relationship.

Damian seemed to want to spend all their free time together, even when he was travelling. He'd made several trips to New

York on business, and since he'd come home from the first trip with a scowl on his face, he'd invited her along on every trip after that. But she'd had to work and couldn't get away, not even once. He'd seemed relatively frustrated with that, but there hadn't been anything she could do about it.

He was scheduled to leave again for a week this afternoon, and Angie knew he was chomping at the bit because he wanted her with him. She admitted to herself that she'd like to go with him on his trip, but she didn't have the vacation time to be with him, and she had to have a job…right?

But it was too soon for anything to change between them; she had the thought even as the memory of last night beat through her veins. His lovemaking hadn't cooled a bit since they'd been together. If anything, it grew fiercer by the day.

Last night at his downtown condo had been…extreme. She blushed hotly just thinking of it. He'd held her pinned to the bedroom wall the first time, and the second time pinned to the side of the bed itself. And if that hadn't been enough, the third time, he'd carried her to the panoramic window that overlooked the city, and stood her on her feet, facing the glass and the gorgeous, evening sky, while he pressed his chest against her back and ordered her to keep her eyes open.

The memory washed over her. The room had been dark. They could see out, but no one would have been able to see in, even if they hadn't been twenty stories high. She'd been overly sensitive from the earlier sessions in his bedroom, but he'd taken his time with her, going down on his haunches and forcing her legs apart while he played with her, readying her for his entry.

He'd stood up, adjusted her stance and plunged in from behind. She'd sucked in a breath as sensation slid down her spine. He'd come twice already in the last couple of hours, so he was leisurely in his seduction. As he moved slowly within her, his hands gripped her hips and his mouth trailed kisses along her neck that landed at her ear. "Are your eyes open?"

"Yes."

"Tell me what you see."

Angie could barely get her thoughts in order as he pushed slowly in and out, moving inexorably within her. "I see…lights. And buildings. Clouds. It's…it's beautiful."

"*You're* beautiful," he whispered. He pushed inside and held himself there, his hands coming in front to cup her breasts, his hands sliding sinuously, almost reverently, back and forth over her skin.

Her breath caught in her throat.

Slowly, he slid the hair back from her ear and whispered, "So, *so* beautiful."

The caress of his voice sent shivers down her spine and she reacted with a small moan.

"I can give you that view, Angie."

Her mind almost splintering with his hands so gentle, she barely comprehended his words. "What?"

"All you have to do is move in here with me," he said softly as his hands ran down her sides and back up again.

"I don't…" Angie couldn't think and her words stumbled to a halt.

His mouth slid to her shoulder and he bit into her flesh as if to subdue her. She didn't need subduing; she was pliant in his arms. He took tiny bites with his teeth, then lifted his mouth and blew on her flesh as if to soothe her. "I love your skin." He licked the spot he'd bitten. "I love your scent, baby. You're so *fucking sweet.*" He pulled his hips back and plunged back inside. "I love it when you come." His mouth moved to her ear and he bit her lobe and his voice when it came was stronger, almost harsh. "I love that you don't say the word 'no' to me."

He pulled out, flipped her around until her naked backside was pressed against the cold glass. He lifted her leg and then he plunged back inside. The sensation of the cold at her back and his heat at her front had the oxygen snarling in her lungs.

He held himself within her and lifted her chin with his fingers until she had no choice but to stare up at him. "I want you to move in here with me. I want you to give up your apartment." The tone of seduction left his voice, his words becoming inflexible in his demand.

As she stared up at him, a current of both pleasure and panic slid through her system. She remained silent, and he continued, "When I get home from work, I want you to be here. I want you to sleep in my bed every night without question. I want to know where you are and that you're safe when I'm not with you."

With his words, his strokes became stronger, more determined, and full-blown arousal came roaring back. His fingers left her chin and together, they looked down at where they were joined. The sight was more than erotic; it was profoundly sexual and within mere minutes, they were exploding in each other's arms as the wave crashed over them both.

In the next moments, he'd carefully released her and balanced her on her feet. He'd led her to the bathroom where he'd cleaned her up gently and patiently. When she'd climbed into bed on legs that trembled, he'd followed her there and had taken her into his arms.

She was lying on her back and he turned to face her. Propping himself up on an elbow, he leaned over her. "I want an answer."

Torn by conflicting feelings, she tried to answer him, "I don't know. It's a lot to think about."

"No, it's not. It's simple…nothing to think about," he shot back, determination lacing his words.

Angie held onto her resolve by thinking of the logistics. "The salon is so far away from here."

His eyes glittered but he remained silent. Watching him, it hit her all at once and she blurted out, "You want me to quit my job."

He inclined his head but said nothing, only continued to watch her with his hawk-like eyes.

"I don't know if I can get another one around here," she replied, knowing damn good and well she was feeling him out, trying to get inside his head to find out what he was thinking.

His eyes narrowed and he began shaking his head, slowly, back and forth.

"I have to work," she said, half-panicked.

He continued to shake his head.

Deep. This shit was getting deep. "I don't have any money. I mean, not enough—"

"You don't need any money, Angie. You don't need anything." His words were firm, ringing with conviction.

She took a stabilizing breath, forcing herself to calm down. "You want to support me?"

"Yes," he replied unequivocally.

"Why?" She couldn't get too excited here. She knew him. This would be nothing more than a convenience for him. It wasn't as if he wanted marriage. He wanted convenience and she needed to remember that.

"Because I want you here," he said tonelessly, as if he was tired of the debate and didn't want her to question him further.

She remained quiet for a moment. "I'll have to think about it."

His eyes had narrowed as if pissed or displeased. He'd rolled over, switched off the lamp and Angie had tossed and turned and had gotten very little sleep at all.

When her cell phone rang, Angie came back to reality. It was Damian's mother, and she slid the bar to answer. She saw the time and knew he'd be boarding a plane for New York about now. They hadn't resolved anything between them last night.

"Hello," she announced, putting the phone between her shoulder and her ear as she used the opportunity to tidy up her station.

"Hi, darling. How are you?"

Guilt rushed through her. She was beside herself...trying to figure out if she should move in with this woman's son. "I'm great," she lied. "And you?"

"Very well. The romance thrives," the older woman said with a hint of humor.

"That is great, then."

"Yes, it is. Listen darling, I'm having a little get together Saturday night and I really, really want you to stop by after you get off work if you can. It's nothing formal...not a sit-down meal. Just drinks and finger foods."

A tiny trickle of unease slid down Angie's spine. Damian wouldn't be there but that shouldn't matter. In fact it should be easier as he still didn't want his mother to know about their relationship.

And besides, Angie liked his mother and was pleased that the older woman seemed to care for her as well. "Sounds fun. Should I bring anything?"

"Not a thing. Now I want to warn you that Damian won't be coming. I don't know if you've spoken to him, but he'll be out of town."

Guilt. Guilt. Guilt. She remained silent and after an abbreviated pause, Mrs. Rule continued, "Anyway, Rick wants to be introduced to a few of my favorite people, and you're on the list, darling. But not only that, he knows you as well so it would be nice for him to see a familiar face, don't you think?"

"That's so sweet. Yeah, I think it's a good idea. Are you sure I can't bring anything?"

"Nothing, darling. Just your sweet little self."

"Okay. So, what does 'nothing formal' mean?" Angie asked.

"It means you can dress however you want. Casual."

"What are you going to wear?" Casual in Angie's world meant blue jeans or shorts. But she didn't think Mrs. Rule's idea of casual was the same.

"I'm going to wear a wrap-dress. I've had it for years but it's a classic. It has good lines…and I feel really good in it. I'm still at that stage in the relationship where I worry over these things."

Angie heard the excitement in the other woman's voice. "Okay, I'll wear a sundress then. How's that?"

"That sounds fine, darling. I know you'll be adorable. I think Courtney mentioned she's going to wear something along the same lines. Now do you remember how to get to the house?"

"Yes, ma'am, I'm sure I'll be able to find it."

Chapter Nine

The rest of the week dragged for Angie. Work was exhausting, and every spare minute she had, she worried about the decision she was going to have to make when Damian returned.

She pretty much already knew that she wanted to move in with him. But she wasn't thrilled about quitting her job. She needed to stand on her own two feet, to make her own money. If something happened to them, if they broke up, she didn't want to be left out in the cold with no income and no place to live.

It occurred to her that she might offer him a compromise. Maybe during the week she could stay at her apartment, but on her days off, she could come stay with him. It wasn't the best idea, but it was all she could come up with. It wasn't really any different than the routine they'd already fallen into, but they'd never acknowledged it out loud.

She held on to the belief that the suggestion might appease him but the text messages she'd received from him during the week made her realize he wouldn't go for the idea.

His first had come the morning after he'd left. *Slept like shit.* She'd sent back a reply: *I'm sorry. Mattress uncomfortable?*

It was fine.

She keyed in a quick response. *I'm sure it's difficult to be away from home.*

His response came back instantaneously. *It's difficult to be away from you.*

Angie read his response and heat bloomed through her veins and in that moment, she decided not to play any more games. *I miss you.*

He hadn't answered, but she figured that he'd either been called away by his business dealings or maybe he thought that his feelings had already been explained. And they had. She knew he missed her.

The next morning his text was more abrasive but no less disconcerting to her. *Why don't you quit that fucking job and catch a flight up here?*

Angie stared at the screen while the blood pumped furiously through her veins. She stalled, not knowing how to answer. Seconds turned into minutes and finally, she keyed, *I can't.*

She hadn't heard from him since.

On Saturday night after work, Angie went home and showered and changed clothes before heading to the Rule household. She'd splurged on a spray-tan the day before, and she felt pretty good in her ankle-length summer sundress and sandals. She'd forgotten what it was like to wear color; leaving the black behind almost felt as if she'd come out of mourning.

When she arrived, the door was opened by a man she recognized. He was the same man who'd pulled Courtney from the last party she'd attended, and there was absolutely no doubt in her mind that he was one of Damian's brothers. With the door wide, he stared at her on the threshold and raised a single eyebrow. A stream of shock slid down her spine. The resemblance was uncanny. Both of these Rule men were tall, dark, and undeniably handsome. They both had dark, wavy hair and their skin tone was almost swarthy, as if they belonged to the great American melting pot of ethnicity.

"Hi," she said, almost stumbling over the word as he continued to stare down at her.

He paused in his perusal, and then pushed the door wide. "Come in."

"Thanks."

As she stepped over the threshold and looked around, he said from behind her, "You belong to Damian."

She stopped short and turned to face him. "I don't really belong to anybody."

"*Right.*"

Before she had time to answer, his mother sailed up with a smile and a champagne glass dangling from her fingers. "Angie, darling." The older woman leaned in and gave Angie an embracing hug that threatened to slosh the liquid from her glass. Angie smiled and hugged her back. "I see you've met my middle son, Nick."

"Oh. Not really." Angie faced the man again and held out her hand, hoping she didn't appear to be as awkward as she felt. "Angie Ross."

He gripped her hand quickly and released her without lingering. "Nick Rule."

Before Angie could say anything more, Justine grabbed her hand and began leading her into the room, while whispering, "He's not for you, darling. We've still got to give Damian time to pull his head from his butt."

The words were so incongruent with the woman's appearance that Angie stumbled and began laughing.

"You think that's funny?"

"Yeah, I do."

"Well, it's true. He needs to realize that you'd be perfect for him, but in the meantime, come and meet Rick's son, Caiden.

He's about your age, maybe a little younger, but he's absolutely adorable."

As Angie was all but dragged across a room full of people and they came to stand in front of Rick and his son, Angie said with a smile, "I already know Rick's son. I'm his stylist, also."

Caiden leaned in and kissed Angie's cheek and then his father followed suit.

"You cut his hair, too?" Mrs. Rule asked and then turned to Rick. "You didn't tell me they knew each other already."

As Angie and Caiden shared a look, she abruptly realized what this was about. Justine was trying to set the two of them up. Would the woman never learn? Finding herself on the receiving end of her manipulations, Angie suddenly realized why his mother drove Damian so crazy.

After chit-chatting a few minutes, the older couple excused themselves and Justine pulled Rick away, undoubtedly trying to give Angie and Caiden some time alone. Angie rolled her eyes and glanced back at Caiden, who she'd known for a good two years. "She's trying to set us up!"

"Actually she's been trying to set me up with every single woman who's here tonight."

"Why?" Angie leaned closer and whispered, "Doesn't she know you're gay?"

He looked taken aback. "Justine? Hell, *my father* doesn't know I'm gay."

Angie glanced back around the room, wondering if she should mind her own business, and saw Courtney speaking to a dark-haired young woman with familiar looking eyes. Caiden noticed her interest and said, "The blonde girl is Courtney, the goddaughter. The brunette is the actual daughter, and her name is Erin."

Angie looked away, not wanting to stare. "I've met Courtney but not Erin."

"Oh, you will. Justine is in her element tonight."

"Don't you like her?" Angie asked, referring to Justine Rule.

"Actually, I do. She's exactly what my father needs, but she is a bit of a match-maker want-to-be, and that's creating a bit of a problem for me."

Angie stopped just short of cringing for the young man and decided she would tell him what she knew, after all. "Hey, let's wander around a bit. I want to tell you something and you may need a bit of privacy for it."

He looked at her with a frown, but he turned and followed her. She stopped and snagged a glass of champagne from a side table, and he did the same. Glancing around as if about to mingle, Angie walked from the room as surreptitiously as possible and headed down a hallway that looked private enough.

She came to an open door that contained a library, and walked inside, Caiden following her. She shut the door and took a sip of the champagne to fortify herself.

"What's up?" he asked.

She attempted to broach the subject slowly. "How long have we known each other?"

He shrugged. "A couple of years, I guess."

She nodded her head and gave him a bittersweet smile. "I like you a lot. I always enjoy cutting your hair. You're cool," she said with a small grin. "I also like your dad."

He frowned as if bracing himself. "Okay?"

"I try to mind my own business, you know?"

Now he was looking really confused. "Spit it out, Angie."

She took a deep breath. "Dude, your father already knows you're gay."

His face paled and he looked cut to the bone. "No way."

She nodded her head sympathetically.

"How do you know?"

She held his eyes as a slice of compassion gentled her voice. "I don't remember the exact conversation. I know it was before I met you. I was cutting your dad's hair one day and he said he had a son who'd just moved back from college and asked me if I could take on another client."

"And?" Caiden prompted.

"I jokingly said something like 'for sure, if he's as good-looking as you are.'"

Angie studied him for a reaction. She didn't know him all that well, but she understood that coming out was something that many people struggled with, especially when it came to their parents.

He winced and asked, "And then?"

"Caiden," she soothed. "It was obvious to me, even then, before I met you, that your father loves you and is proud of you. All he said was, 'Well, my son looks just like me, but don't get your hopes up, the kid's gay.'" Angie gave him a smile to take away any sting her words may have imparted and then continued, "He said it with so much pride, like you were the light of his life and could do no wrong. It's never occurred to me before tonight that you didn't know that he already knew."

He stumbled back a step and fell onto the sofa. Angie followed to sit beside him, and picked up his hand, patting it gently.

※

Damian walked through the airport parking lot and climbed into his car. He started the motor just as his cell phone rang.

He let the engine idle as he answered the call. "What's up?" he questioned shortly, wanting nothing more than to get back to Angie as quickly as possible.

"And good-*fucking*-evening to you too, big brother," Nick snarled sarcastically.

Damian blew out a breath and attempted a more reasonable tone, even as he put the call on speaker and began to drive. "What's going on, Nick?"

"Where are you? Still in New York?" Nick asked in his usual bored tone of voice.

Damian glanced at the clock on the dash. "No. I'm home. Leaving the airport now."

"Very good. *You* can handle this shit," his brother said curtly.

Irritation bled down Damian's spine. "What shit, exactly?"

"Our dear mother is having a party right about now—"

Irritation turned into frustrated anger. *"Fuck, no."*

"Give me a minute. You're going to want to hear what I have to say," Nick replied as if privy to something of importance.

"And what would that be?" Damian asked with little patience.

"Your woman is here," Nick announced blandly.

"My woman?" Damian asked with a snarl.

"That's what I said, yes."

An edge of aggression raised his hackles. "How do you know about my woman?"

"I saw her here at the last party. She's the one you brought who apparently has you so fucked up that you think nobody notices when you drop off the face of the earth?"

"You're imagining things again, Nick," he denied, not wanting his brother butting into his personal business. "And you weren't even at the last party."

"I may not have shown my face, but I was there. And I saw your woman. I'm referring to the little gothic chick who's not a gothic chick anymore?"

At that spot on description, Damian's nerves took a leap. "What about her?" As he boarded the freeway, sudden tension made him head toward his mother's house instead of Angie's. Even though he didn't care for it, he acknowledged that Nick obviously knew more than Damian thought he did.

"As I was saying, she's here and she is, at this moment, sequestered in the library with a man who, as we both know, isn't you," Nick said in such a over-exaggerated, know-it-all tone that Damian wanted to plant his fist in his brother's face.

Coupled with the need to smack Nick, Damian felt such a vicious jolt of jealousy that he almost swerved the car. He took three deep breaths and concentrated on his driving.

When Damian was silent, Nick continued, "Are you on your way?"

"What do you think?" Damian snarled.

"All right then. I'll see you in a few."

"Nick, wait," Damian interjected.

"What?"

"What exactly were you going to do if I was still in New York?"

"That's an easy one, big brother. Whatever the fuck you instructed me to do. I've got your back."

Damian let out a breath. "Yeah."

His brother ended the call and Damian did the same.

Damian walked through his mother's home without giving anyone time to engage him in conversation. He saw Nick hovering over Courtney with a pissed-off expression on his face. He continued trekking across the room with a solitary purpose. He met his brother's stare only briefly, but it was long enough for Nick to motion with a tilt of his head toward the library, telling Damian that Angie was still in there.

He cracked his knuckles and continued crossing the carpet without breaking stride. He came to the library door and without knocking, twisted the handle and stepped inside.

He walked all the way into the room on silent feet and came up behind the sofa. Angie and the unknown man were sitting side-by-side, holding hands, heads together, engrossed in low-pitched conversation.

Rage, unlike any he'd ever experienced shot down his spine and then clawed back up his throat. He paced around to the front of the sofa and stood, his muscles braced for attack.

Angie glanced up, and more slowly, so did the young man she sat with. He was a good-looking kid, ridiculously so, and Damian about came unglued. "You have two fucking seconds, Angie. Start talking, now."

***

Angie paled when she saw the look in Damian's eyes. She'd seen him angry before, of course, but nothing to compare to this. There was no other word for it; he was incensed. Alarm trickled through her veins. "I thought you were out of town."

He took a step forward, aggression in every line of his body. *"Wrong answer, babe."*

At Damian's mounting fury, Angie felt Caiden jerk beside her and begin to stand up in a bid to extricate himself from her. But she continued to hold his hand, pulling on it, trying to keep him seated. Absolutely nothing good could come of him standing up in front of an enraged Damian, even if only to try to sidestep him. She attempted to speak, "This…this is Caiden. He's Rick's son."

"I don't give a fuck whose son he is." Damian transferred his glare to the young man sitting next to her. "Let go of her hand. *Now.* Or I'll do it for you."

Caiden started shaking her hand off of his, no doubt understanding that Damian's rage was a direct result of Angie sitting with him. Angie let him have his hand back and then she jumped to her feet and stood between the two men. "I'm glad you're home," she said to Damian, attempting to cool him down. "Caiden was just leaving," she added quickly, trying to protect the younger man.

Damian stood still, his muscles tensing. "No, he wasn't."

She tried to control the butterflies pushing through her stomach. "What's that supposed to mean?"

"It means he can stay exactly where he's at until I decide if I'm going to let him live or not."

"Damian—" Angie began.

"Oh, for God's sake, Angie," Caiden interjected from where he still sat on the sofa. "Tell him the truth."

Damian's eyes narrowed, the veins in his neck bulged, and he looked ready to flip a switch. Angie glanced down at Caiden. "Don't make it worse—"

"I'm trying to make it better. We don't need any animosity here. Jesus Christ, my father's probably going to marry his mother—"

"*What?*" Damian shouted, turning an even colder shade of pissed.

"Damian!" Angie screamed, "Calm down!"

Damian clenched his fists. "I want to know why you're in here with him, alone, and somebody best start with some satisfactory answers or there's going to be hell to pay," he threatened, pulling her within the circle of his arms as he spoke. He spun her around, until her back was pressing against his chest and his arms around her waist were like bands of steel. Angie couldn't see him in this position, but she knew his next words were directed to Caiden. "You see her, asshole?"

Angie almost cringed when she saw Caiden's face pale. "I see her."

"She's mine," Damian hissed with barely controlled violence.

Caiden wore an expression that clearly said he couldn't believe what was going down. "Dude, I don't want her."

After that, everything happened at once.

The library door opened, and both Damian's mother and Rick walked inside. Damian didn't even seem to notice as his attention stayed focused on Caiden. "No? Why the fuck were you holding onto her hand like you had a goddamn right to it?" At the same time Damian growled the question, Angie felt a strong surge of testosterone rise up within his muscles and she knew he was about to set her aside and make a lunge for Caiden.

Caiden must have felt the imminent threat as well, because he opened his mouth to begin defending himself. Angie knew what words were about to come from his lips; he was about to tell Damian the truth about his sexuality, but he never had the chance.

Rick took in the scene with a single glance and strode over until he stood just beside the couch, next to his son. Angie knew what he was seeing, what he was hearing, what Damian's mother was seeing as well. It must have been clear to everyone in the room that Damian and Angie's relationship was *anything* but casual. *Busted.* Damian had his arms wrapped around her as if he owned her and everything about her.

Angie knew without looking that the jealousy she could hear in Damian's voice had to be reflected on his face and in his physical bearing. So, it was no surprise when Rick snarled at Damian, *"Back off."* With that, he placed his hand on Caiden's shoulder in a defensive posture and continued to stare Damian down. "My son isn't interested in your woman. He's gay. Leave him the fuck alone."

Angie felt the tension slowly drain from Damian's body, but then another more subtle kind of nerves took over his system. The immediate threat to *his woman* neutralized, Angie knew that Damian was now taking in the dynamics of the other people in the room and what that meant to him.

Caiden glanced up at his father and his father down at him, and suddenly, Angie realized they were being made privy to a meeting that should be private.

Caiden rose to his feet, and after an abbreviated, awkward moment, he and Rick embraced.

When they'd released each other, Damian cleared his throat and questioned, "You're gay?" Angie froze in his arms and with a reaction she couldn't control, shoved her arm backward until her elbow made a satisfying thump into Damian's abdomen.

Caiden saw the motion, smiled, and nodded his head. "Angie and I are only friends." He held Damian's eyes as if feeling him out, and then, cautiously, he held out his hand. "Caiden Harris."

Damian retained one arm around Angie, reciprocating with his right hand. "Damian Rule."

The two men shook hands. From Angie's new viewpoint by Damian's side, she saw when he then held his hand out to Rick, but it wasn't automatically taken.

Rick crossed his arms over his chest and scowled at Damian. Then he transferred his gaze to Angie, and with a very paternal expression on his face, he asked, "Are you okay?"

"I'm fine," she said with a small smile. "This is Damian," she said to Rick, trying again to get him to shake Damian's hand, "he's Justine's oldest son."

"I figured as much," Rick said as he finally shook Damian's hand, but with little warmth. "You go off a bit half-cocked with no real justification, don't you?" Rick challenged as Justine Rule slid up next to him.

She'd been standing close to the library door taking everything in, but now she stood next to Rick and studied her son as if he'd grown an extra head. She looked between Damian and Angie, back and forth and then again as if truly stumped. "I'm trying to figure this out."

When Damian shrugged his shoulders in silence, his mother turned to Rick and changed the direction of the conversation, if only for a moment. "Why didn't you tell me your son is gay? Don't you think it might have saved him an uncomfortable experience? I didn't *have* to try to match him up with every single woman here tonight." Without waiting for an answer, she turned to Caiden, "I'm sorry, darling."

"It's no problem. I understand. And as Angie has known me for a while," he shot a dark look at Damian, "it's not that big of a deal."

Being reminded of Angie made Damian's mother turn in their direction again with a quizzical frown. "Angie darling, have you been lying to me by omission?"

Angie took a deep breath and confessed, "Yes, ma'am. I'm sorry."

"Well, you're forgiven of course, but why would you do that?" Before Angie could form an answer, Mrs. Rule glanced at Damian. "Never mind, darling. I know why you did it." The older woman looked a little hurt, and Damian had the good grace to flush.

"Mother," Damian began, and then cleared his throat.

"Yes?" his mother asked, as if her feelings weren't hurt at all.

Damian glanced at the other two men in the room, and Angie knew that neither one of them was ready to take pity on him and leave—not after the way he'd acted. Looking back to his mother, he said, "I'm sorry that I misled you."

"Misled, darling?" she prompted in the most genteel voice that Angie had ever heard.

"I'm sorry I lied to you," Damian qualified.

Mrs. Rule inclined her head graciously and Damian continued, "I'd like to introduce you once again, to Angie Ross, my... my—"

Mrs. Rule schooled her features into a perfectly neutral expression and Angie cracked up on the inside as she and the older woman shared a quick peek at each other before his mother asked, "Your what, Damian?"

Damian knew he'd been made, that much was evident by the look on his face. "My woman. My girlfriend. My better half." He stopped speaking and pulled Angie all the way back into his arms again before continuing, "The woman who drives me crazy. The woman who makes me want to kill innocent men." Angie was experiencing a hot rush of butterflies in her stomach while Damian threw a look at Caiden. "Sorry about that." Caiden shrugged and Damian looked back to his mother. "How much more do you want me to say? She's the reason I'm not interested in any of the women you throw in my direction, she's the reason I cut my trip short by three days." He took a deep breath. "Is that enough or do you want me to go on? She's the one who calms me down, makes me happy, sleeps in my—"

Justine Rule held up her hand. "That's enough, darling. Your mother gets the picture," she said humorously. With that, she went to Damian and Angie stepped aside as Mrs. Rule hugged her son and then hugged Angie in turn. "Now that wasn't so bad, was it?" She asked them both.

Angie responded with a smile and shook her head, but Damian only grimaced.

Justine turned to the group as a whole. "We've gotten a lot cleared up tonight. I won't be trying to fix Caiden up anymore. Well, at least not with any women," she said with a smile in his direction, "and I'll try not to mess up in the future with any of my other children as I did with Damian. It's best that I just stay out of their personal lives, I think. I was going to try to get Courtney and Nick together, but I've learned from my mistakes. Instead, I'll leave my son alone and find some other nice young men for her to choose from."

"Mother—" Damian began to interject.

"What, darling?"

"Never mind. I'm sure you know what's best."

"I'm sure I do."

Chapter Ten

After the party, as they both had their vehicles, Damian followed Angie to her apartment. He thought about the scene in the library during the entire drive. For what it was worth, he supposed his mother had been right. *It hadn't been that bad.*

His mother knew about them now, and as she liked Angie, it finally dawned on him that now she'd really leave him alone; she wouldn't try her damn matchmaking skills anymore.

And that had to be a good thing.

So why did he still feel as if he had acid burning in his stomach that wouldn't go away?

He continued to contemplate the matter. Maybe it had worked out. Maybe he'd had nothing to be upset about to begin with. The dude had been gay. But Damian had had thirty minutes to stew after his brother's phone call and warning. He'd had half an hour to imagine the worst-case scenario, which was Angie, with another man.

The burn in his stomach intensified. He tried to breathe it out. As he parked the car and followed Angie upstairs, he tried to reason with himself. It had been a simple misunderstanding.

A miscommunication. That was all. She hadn't done anything wrong, she hadn't been unfaithful in any way.

So why the hell was he so keyed up?

Deep down, he knew the answer. It was because he didn't have the right. He didn't have a one-hundred percent, no questions asked, no holes barred, absolute, unequivocal right to Angie's thoughts. To her body. To her person.

And that's what he wanted.

That's what the fuck he wanted with her.

And there was only one way he was going to get it.

So, he'd start work on that problem tomorrow. But for now, it had been four days since he'd had her alone. Four days since he'd held her naked. Four days since he'd pushed inside and demanded her complete surrender.

Yeah. *Fuck yeah.* Everything else could wait. He wanted what he wanted and he wanted it now.

He was acting like he was still pissed but Angie didn't think he was. But he was definitely behaving differently.

She'd expected him to follow her up to her apartment and lay down his ultimatum that she move in with him. She knew that was what he wanted, but that wasn't what he seemed interested in at the moment.

Granted, it had been four days since they'd seen each other.

She had a clear view from where she stood at the dinette as he shut and bolted the front door. He reached down and pulled the polo over his head and tossed it aside. Her eyes dropped to the ridges of his abdomen and she sucked in a breath. *He kept getting hotter every freakin' day.*

He pushed off his shoes and socks, and pulled the belt from around his waist, letting it drop to the floor. Without taking his eyes from her, he crossed the few steps until he was in standing directly in front of her. Encircling her wrist with his fingers, he pulled her into the bedroom and over to the bed.

Angie licked her lips as fire swept through her body. "You've got a one-track mind tonight, don't you?"

"I don't know, do I?" he asked softly, almost dangerously.

She swallowed deeply and nodded her head.

Reaching for her hips, he lifted her dress to her waist and pulled her panties down and off. Tossing them aside, he tipped her chin up with one finger. "Let's talk about what you did tonight. We'll start with the good shit." His eyes held hers as he ran his fingers into her hair, in a clasp that held her captive. "I've thought this through and I realize you were alone with him because of what my mother did. She'd been throwing women at him the entire night, right?"

When Angie nodded her head, he continued, "So you were comforting him, because you were the only one who knew he was gay, is that right?"

She cleared her throat. "Yeah, pretty much. I was also telling him that his father already knows about his sexuality. I sort of figured out that Caiden didn't think his father knew he was gay and I was, you know, breaking the news to him."

"Well, that was a compassionate thing to do," he said, after a pause, but in a monotone voice.

"I think so," she said with a hint of defensiveness. "I had to debate about it for a bit."

Damian continued, "So I want you to know that I appreciate how sweet you are. What a good person you are—"

Angie could feel it coming. "But?"

"But, the thing is, I don't give *a rat's ass if he's gay*. Granted, the fact that he's gay is the only thing that saved him from going to the emergency room tonight, but as far as you're concerned, you can't be alone with him. Him or any other gay man. You got that?"

"Why?" she questioned.

"*Why?*" he asked as if he hadn't heard her correctly.

"Yes, why?"

His fingers tightened in her scalp. "Because gay men have penises. They have balls." His voice hardened, "Too many of them are bisexual. Trust me, if any woman in the world could turn a gay man straight, it would be you, baby."

Angie stood within his grasp and listened in amazement. It was obvious to her that his opinion came from a heterosexual viewpoint. A very hetero viewpoint. *So* hetero that he was unable to see that gay men were just that, gay. She could *try* to explain it to him, she could argue that just as he wasn't sexually interested in other men, gay men weren't sexually interested in women. But the problem was, Angie knew it would go in one ear and out the other. Damian wouldn't get it. Not because he wasn't intelligent, but because he was so *male*.

She remained silent as all of that ran through her head and he continued, "Besides, let's talk about the party for a minute." His mouth flattened. "Suppose a straight man saw you walk off with him, undoubtedly to be alone. Suppose that straight man didn't know the guy was gay. You know what he would think?"

"What would he think?" she asked, wondering at the depth of how Damian's mind worked.

"He'd think that you were up for grabs. He'd think that maybe he had a chance at you, too." His expression clouded in anger. "So, next thing you know, you've got straight men hitting up on you because they think you're available."

"Damian—"

"*Be careful, Angie,*" he warned softly.

"You're taking this a little too far," she argued.

"Am I?"

She nodded her head.

"I don't think so." His chin jutted out. "I'm telling you how I feel, I'm telling you what I expect." He pushed forward, his torso aligning with hers in a sharp movement. "And I'm telling you that you can't be alone with *any man*. Not one. Not a single fucking man is acceptable."

"My father—"

"*Fine*. Your father," he spit out. "If I ever meet him, I'll have to trust him not to be a perverted fuck. But nobody else. Gay is not an excuse to be alone with a man, already married is for damn fucking sure not an excuse. *No-fucking-body* gets to be alone with you, understand me?"

She stared at him and he kept talking. "If I catch you alone with a man again, I'm going to beat the living shit out of him, and you—"

"What about me, Damian?" She questioned him without moving a muscle. She was absolutely enthralled but she wasn't going to admit it. "What would you do?"

"You're about to find out, baby."

With the threat hanging between them, Angie didn't have long to wait for Damian's next move. He reached down, and with one fell swoop, he peeled her sundress over her head and dropped it to the floor. As the dress was lined and he'd already taken her underwear, she stood naked except for her high heels. Her pulse quivered and picked up speed as he stared down at her bare skin. A rush of blood tinged his face as a tic began beating erratically in his cheek.

His hands fell to her waist and he pulled her hips into his with a quick show of aggression. "You know what four fucking days without you does to me?"

As his hands slid down and bit into her hips, a rush of wet heat pooled between her thighs. "Turns you into a mad man?" she managed.

His hands moved back up, following the curve of her waist, and then caressed back down again. "You think it's funny, but I'm telling you it's unacceptable." As he spoke, his nostrils flared and he let go of her with one hand to begin removing the rest of his clothing. He pushed his pants and boxers down with one quick motion and stepped out of them. Completely naked now, his hands fell back to her hips and his erection sprang up between them.

Reaching up with one strong hand, he wrapped it around the back of her neck and squeezed, pulling her hair and pressing her chin up so he could reach her lips. He stared down into her eyes with burning need. "You don't have a fucking clue how I feel about you, do you?"

Her lungs seized up and her heart almost stopped beating. She became paralyzed with anticipation and need.

"There's a reason I get so crazy." His pupils dilated. "There's a reason I'm so fucked-up about you."

Angie's breath hitched as she continued to stare into his eyes while she tried not to faint. His words stalled and her pulse beat loudly in her ears as she waited.

His hands clenched around her and with a sudden growl from deep in his chest, he picked her up, dropped her to the bed and came over her, pushing his legs between her thighs and pressing his torso against hers. Grabbing her hands in his, he spread his fingers through hers until their palms were pressed together. He raised them over her head and held her hands to the mattress. A wave of dizzy delight rushed down her spine. He transferred both hands to one of his and brought the other down between them, where he guided his penis to her wet opening.

His erection pulsed threateningly between them, right at the very core of her as he held her eyes. As he watched her, and as she waited with breathless anticipation, he pressed forward until the head of his erection was inside. Pleasure screamed through her bloodstream and she began to close her eyes.

He nudged her hands and pushed his hips, bringing him further inside by another degree. "Open your eyes."

Her lids flew open and she panted, waiting, breathless.

"Why do you drive me so fucking crazy, Angie?"

She shook her head against the pillow. "I don't know."

He growled and pushed inside another inch, bringing him to the point in her channel where he stretched her the most. "Yes, you do," he asserted.

His voice lowered and his expression almost gentled. "You know why I'm insane around you." His eyes dropped but they didn't close all the way as he pulled his hips back and with one long, steady stroke, he impaled her. The depth of his pleasure was there for her to see as his eyes rolled to the back of his head. His reaction was involuntary and it sent a reflexive answer through her.

A hot fierce ache blossomed inside, easing his way.

He shuddered and then seemed to find his control as he began moving his hips back and forth, plunging inside and out again in a rhythm that was utterly intoxicating to her already sensitized nerve endings.

His eyes stayed hot on hers as her orgasm began to build. He was absolutely beautiful as primitive hunger filled his expression. *It was for her. She knew it was. She could feel it.*

As sexual and emotional pleasure invaded her senses, she couldn't stand it anymore. She began going over the edge as passion built and she began to see an explosion of colors. She let out a soft wail, and as she began climaxing within his embrace, he stiffened against her and began pumping with stronger, more heated strokes.

He released her hands and lifted her chin as he thrust in and out. He gripped her chin and bared his teeth as he hissed out in a tone of reverence, "It's because I love you."

Her world exploded and his did the same as his seed shot out and erupted within her. Waves of pleasure rushed over her as his words penetrated her brain. They rode out the rest of their orgasm, and then he fell on top of her, just barely holding himself up enough so that she could breathe.

She concentrated on inhaling and exhaling, while stars danced in her head and a thrilling rush of delight pounded through her veins.

After a minute or so, he raised himself back up and over her. His eyes clashed with hers and he studied her intently. He examined her thoroughly, and at her silence, any residual pleasure in his expression began to dissolve. Before that could happen, Angie locked her hands around his neck and held him in place.

Holding his eyes with hers, she took a leap of faith and said, "I love you, too."

A shudder racked his frame as he took a deep breath. He closed his eyes and muttered, "Thank God."

He opened his eyes again and began nodding his head with a look of satisfaction. "Okay. That's good."

An arrow of delight pierced her heart. "Yeah, it is."

He reached down and kissed her, long and leisurely, and then he raised his head and looked at her with a new gleam in his eye. "Time for round two, baby."

Her eyes flared and she smiled spontaneously, giving him all the permission he needed.

When Angie woke up, she anticipated a lazy Sunday morning. But when she reached her hand out, Damian wasn't there. He'd kept her awake until almost dawn punishing her in the most pleasurable way possible, just as he'd threatened, and now, she almost freaked when she saw the time.

It was noon already.

Pushing the covers aside to get out of bed, she saw his note. *Went to grab us something to eat.* She had no idea what time he'd left, but she hurried through her shower. She was just finishing putting on her clothes when she heard him walk back in. Wishing she'd had time for at least a touch of make-up, she walked out to the living room.

She stood in the doorway as he dropped his keys and the take-out containers on the kitchen counter. Glancing up, he studied her in silence for a moment. "Hey."

"Hey," she said softly. The words they'd spoken last night hadn't been repeated, but she didn't think that meant the feelings had disappeared.

"I brought food," he said with a hesitant tone in his voice that she couldn't ever remember hearing from him before.

She nodded her head and then cleared her throat. "I read your note."

His eyes never left hers as he came around the counter and leaned against it. He crossed his arms over his chest and studied her.

As she stood across the space that divided them, the look on his face make the blood rush to her head, making her dizzy. She swallowed and locked her knees. *Something was about to happen.* Was he about to lay down an ultimatum about her moving in with him?

He ran his fingers through his hair and she saw his hand shake. Her stomach knotted up with a mirroring sensation. His eyes dropped to her bare legs and then lifted again. Tension filled his muscles and his voice when it came out didn't hold its usual commanding strength. "I can't keep on like this, Angie. It's driving me insane. I know you think it's probably too soon, but I seriously *cannot* live without you."

A sharp, fierce hit of joy held her in its grip as she waited.

He pushed off the counter and tracked toward her. Reaching down, he lifted her chin. "I'm about to do something that's scaring me shitless." He clenched his jaw. "If you blow me off, if you say 'no', I'm going to die. I just want you to know that." His thumb slid across her bottom lip and his voice gentled a bit as a half-smile crossed his features. "But no pressure, okay?"

"Okay," she whispered and tried to breathe so she wouldn't pass out. *Holy. Shit. Holy shit...Holy shit.*

He slid his thumb back and forth over her bottom lip and abruptly, a kind of peace settled over his features. "I love you."

She bit her lip and sudden tears washed her eyes. "I love you, too."

"So much, baby," he whispered, his thumbs reaching out to brush her tears away.

They continued to stare at each other, the emotional connection strong between them, and then he put his hand in his pocket and pulled out a small, square box. Angie looked down and gasped and the tears started flowing more freely.

He dropped to one knee and took her left hand in his. She stared down in shaken joy as he opened the box and showed her the ring inside. A large, brilliant, square-cut diamond sat in a blaze of glory on a bed of dark blue velvet. Her heart stalled before beginning a cadence in triple time. He picked the ring out of the box and held it poised over her left ring finger.

He looked back up and his eyes blazed into hers. "Angie. I love you," he repeated.

She was beyond speech and she nodded her head.

Studying her intently, he asked, "Will you be my wife?"

Joy rushed over her as she began nodding her head frantically. Relief, sharp and forceful, took over his features as he pushed the ring onto her finger. He held her hand tightly in his and then leaned down and sealed a kiss over the finger that held his ring.

As she tried to get her tears under control, he stood back up to his full height and enclosed her within a strong embrace. He rocked her gently, to and fro and then stopped and tipped her face to his. "Is it what you want?" he asked with just a trace of a worried frown.

"Oh, God, *yes,*" she said.

He smiled and kissed her forehead and told her the same thing he'd been telling her all along, "It's going to be good, baby."

Epilogue

The intercom on Damian's desk buzzed and he felt mildly irritated at the interruption, which was immediately mitigated with subtle anticipation when his imagination supplied him with a picture of Angie. *Would his little witch come today?*

The coolly enunciated voice of his secretary filled the room. "Mr. Rule, your wife is here to see you."

The words sent a direct hit to Damian's groin. "Send her in."

He set his pen down and stood to his feet in a fluid motion. Striding around his desk, he leaned against it and waited. His pulse hammered loudly in his ears as the promise of what awaited him filled his blood with heat.

The door clicked open and Angie peeked into the room before walking just inside and shutting the door behind her. Turning to face him, she leaned back against the solid wood panel and waited, a placid, neutral expression on her face that Damian knew was costing her to maintain.

As he ran his eyes down the beige, nondescript trench coat she wore, which landed a few inches above stiletto heels, Damian experienced a sharp, piercing arrow of arousal that mixed with appalled consternation. She remained silent and he narrowed his eyes as he tried not to let the censure or the lust bleed into his voice. "Lock the door."

With hands that shook, she fumbled behind her and slid the bolt into place.

A savage hit of primitive hunger clawed in his gut and blended with the maddening displeasure gripping him by the throat. "We've got a problem, baby."

She took a deep breath and blew it out as she held his eyes. Lifting her chin in challenge, she ran her eyes down to the bulge in his pants before locking onto his gaze once again. "Do we?"

He continued to stare her down as he nodded his head. "The trench coat leads me to believe that you're naked underneath, and while I have to admit it's a highly intoxicating thought, I'm reminding myself that *you know better.*" He raised a single eyebrow as his muscles clenched. "You best *not* have driven across the city, walked across the parking lot and ridden up in the elevator butt-assed naked."

Color highlighted her cheekbones with a hint of sexual arousal that she couldn't hide from him. "I'm not butt-assed naked," she denied softly.

"You best not be, Angie."

"I'm not," she answered as she shook her head. She motioned to the coat she wore as the silky waves of her hair curled around her shoulders and forced his abdominal muscles into bands of steel as he imagined sinking his hands through the tresses and holding her imprisoned. As he formed a mental image of holding her spread-eagle over his desk, her fingers came up to the belt of her coat and she released it. As he held himself impossibly still, almost too scared to move, she shrugged her shoulders and the coat fell to the floor. She sidestepped the material, braced herself against the wall and breathed softly, "Now I'm naked."

Damian tensed and felt the sucker-punch directly where she aimed it. Waves of undiluted lust screamed down his spine and his cock hardened to its fullest. Except for the stilettos, she was completely, undeniably naked, not even a tiny scrap of lace panties for covering.

As he stared at her, looking her over from top to bottom, he could feel her hesitancy about what she'd done. She had no way of knowing exactly how he'd react, and she was taking a chance with his always-volatile emotions where she was concerned.

And he was pissed, no question of that. But he was also so fucking turned on that he didn't know how much longer he was going to be able to contain his emotions. A voracious urge beating through his blood, he watched as she shifted restlessly when he continued to stand completely still. She sucked in a breath, her palms flattened against the wall beside her, and the feminine muscles of her abdomen jumped and quivered.

Another wave of blood rushed to his cock as he pushed off the desk and started forward.

"The twins are in school?" he knew they were, but he liked to have everything organized inside his brain before he let go and let the purely physical animal inside of him take over.

She nodded her head and expelled a provocative breath as he paced across the room with a steady stride.

"You still having a hard time adjusting now that they're in first grade? It's been three weeks, baby."

"You know that I miss them," she whispered as she watched him approach.

He reached down and snatched up her wrists and brought them over her head in a move that held her prisoner. "You want to start on the next one, then?"

He slid his thigh between her legs and pushed it against her mound and her eyes dilated and her breath caught in her throat. "Maybe," she whispered on a gasp.

"I thought we wanted another one," he said as he leaned down and bit her bottom lip, letting it go just as quickly as he'd raked it between his teeth.

Her breath hitched again and she said, "We do."

"But?"

Her eyes held his, her lids drooping with a sensual aura that was so addicting he could barely keep from baring his teeth in aggression. Her words when she answered came out shaky, "I don't feel like a mommy right now."

"No? What do you feel like?" he asked, one hand enclosing both of her wrists as his free hand dropped down to encapsulate a soft, white breast.

"Your wife," she said huskily.

"Do you now?" he teased darkly, fire rushing up his spine, making the anticipation of the moment almost more than he could stand.

She nodded her head and he tightened his fingers that held her wrists captive. He pushed his torso into hers, threatening her with his masculine strength. *"My* wife would know better than to drive across town naked," he said, getting back to the reason that tension still held him in its grip. He pumped against her, while he focused his gaze on her eyes. *"Tell me the truth."*

She licked her lips and swirled her hips in a tiny circle, silently begging him for more. "They're in my bag."

"What's in your bag?"

"My clothes. I changed in the restroom in your waiting area."

For the first time, Damian noticed the oversized purse she'd carried in and that now lay in a neglected heap beside her feet. His emotions shifted, and the residual anger he'd felt dissipated and fled completely as his appreciation of her feminine impulse to please him sent his addiction for her up another notch. "Good girl." He pinched her nipple and rolled it between his fingers. "You're sweet, you know that?"

Her hips became almost frantic and he couldn't wait another second. Picking her up at the hips, he carried her across the room and spread her across his desk. He pushed her thighs wide, and came between them. He released his belt and zipper, and plunged inside, all the way in, with one smooth stroke.

She let out a gasp as her hands came to his shoulders and clutched at him. Her fevered impatience sent a lick of heat that manifested itself in the thrusts of his hips, stroking in and out with a rhythm that he knew would drive her to the edge.

He needed her at the edge, because he was about to lose it. Even after so many years, it never let up with her. His need, the fire he had for her that always smoldered just beneath the surface. As he kept up a steady pumping motion, his hand slid up and his fingers entangled in her hair, with a need to possess. Her eyes flew open and she let out a shallow, ragged sound as their glances clashed and held.

Her nostrils flared and she let out another tiny moan. His fingers fisted more tightly. Her eyes widened and she took in a ragged breath. "I love you," she moaned as she lifted her hips.

A hot, fierce ache built in his loins. "I love you, too. *Forever,*" he groaned as his lips fell to hers. He kissed her deeply and as their tongues swirled, he felt it the moment that the pleasure took hold of them both. He lifted his head and found her watching him, the heat so strong in her eyes that he snapped. Inundated with both love and lust, he gripped her to him and went over the edge.

She screamed his name and flew over the precipice with him.

His torso fell to hers and they lay together until their breathing calmed. He picked himself up and propped himself on his elbows.

Her eyes glittered with a feminine radiance. "Happy birthday," she said softly.

He leaned in and kissed her, once, on the lips. "Best birthday present ever."

She hit him on the shoulder. "You knew I wouldn't have driven across the city in nothing but a trench coat."

He shrugged a shoulder. "You had me wondering, baby."

Her teasing smile dissolved and a serious look colored her eyes. "Did you mean it?"

"Mean what?"

"You think we should try for a third?"

"Yeah, absolutely. I still want another one. Don't you? You haven't changed your mind, have you?"

She shook her head. "I'm ready."

He smiled, a feeling of satisfaction holding him in its grip. "I think it's time. I know the girls will be thrilled to have a baby to play with."

"What if it's not a boy?" she asked with worry in her voice.

He shrugged as if unconcerned. "Then it will be a girl."

"You don't mind?"

"You know I don't care either way." He reached down and brushed his lips across her forehead. "All I want is for you and the kids to be safe and healthy." He spread his fingers through her hair and studied her intently. "That's all that matters to me."

She smiled that special smile that she reserved just for him and his heart turned over. "I love you so much," she whispered.

He leaned down and kissed her lips, gently but with pure possession. "I love you, too, babe. So much you'll never know."

THE END

Excerpt from Nick and Courtney's story:

Rule's Property

(Book Two, The House of Rule)

Rule's Property

Nick's arms came over his chest and he crossed them again in impatience. "How many more months? Three?"

Courtney knew what he was asking. She'd be finished with college in three months. "Yeah."

"What are your plans? You're coming home, right?"

The word 'home' had been confusing to Courtney for a while now. Was Florida not her home anymore? Was her home now in Missouri? Really, the only place she wanted to be was where Nick was. But she couldn't be too apparent to him. It was bad enough that he knew that she'd missed him so much that she'd manipulated him to come see her. "Yeah, probably."

"Probably? What does that mean?" his voice sharpened in question.

"I need to find a job. If possible, I want to be in a place that's familiar to me. That's either Florida or Missouri."

"St. Louis," he narrowed it down emphatically.

She nodded her head, but negated that with, "Maybe."

With her answer, he pushed off the wall and headed toward her. Her stomach clenched with hot anticipation. His footsteps stalled when he was less than two feet away and he seemed to shake himself. His features became strained as he held himself in suspended motion. "You promised me you'd come back to St. Louis."

"I know."

"You need to make good on that. Your promise was the only reason I let you leave."

At the look in his eyes, she knew she had to try to reason with him. "Nick," she began slowly, "You didn't *let* me leave. I was never yours to control." She studied him, noting the anger that spread across his face at her words. She continued, trying to temper her voice, "I *want* to come back to St. Louis. If I don't get a job here, then after graduation, I'll—"

He cut her off when he stepped into her personal space with a glare. "Not mine?" She backed up a step and he followed her until she bumped into the back of the sofa. He didn't touch her but the threat was there. When she came to a halt, he repeated incredulously, *"Not mine?"* and reached down and lifted the necklace that she always wore from around her neck. Her heart beat loudly in her ears as he gripped the charm that dangled from it. His eyes narrowed and he asked for the third time, "Not mine?"

The oxygen stuck in her throat and she shook her head, as she remained trapped by his gaze.

He tilted his head as if in sarcastic question. "If you don't belong to me, who the hell do you think you belong to?" he asked in a far-too soft voice that didn't reflect any gentleness.

When she remained mute, he continued, "I don't see anybody else taking care of you. I don't see anybody else flying halfway across the country to make sure you're all right and that there's no mother-fucker taking advantage of you." He sucked in oxygen. "And who, exactly, do you think pays your bills?"

She swallowed and leaned away from him, feeling the pull from the chain around her throat, but he didn't let go. She glanced down at the tendons corded in his neck and then back up to the fire in his eyes as he continued, "Who do you think paid for these useless little pajamas you're wearing? Who do you think pays for *all* your clothes, the food you eat, the allowance you get?" His eyes held hers with ruthless intent. "Who do you think paid for that pretty little car you drive?"

Guilt running through her from all the things his family had supplied, she licked her lips and whispered, "The corporation."

He began shaking his head as if she had it all wrong and a new agitation took hold of her senses. "Not the company?" she asked quietly.

"Nope. Not the company." His eyes blistered into hers. "Me. Just me."

"Wh—why?" she stuttered. "I don't understand."

"Nothing to understand, sweetheart. Damian assumed responsibility for Erin. You came next and I got you."

"Got me?"

"Figure of speech. I took responsibility for your upkeep."

Courtney began to hear a fine buzzing in her head. "Justine—"

He cut off her question. "Doesn't have any money of her own. Doesn't own the company. Our father died mired in debt. What you see, we built from scratch, the three of us. Any money our mother has comes from us."

Her heartbeat stalled before picking up again, running at triple speed, at the new insight.

Still holding the charm with one hand, he lifted the other and ran a single finger down her cheekbone in a gentle, yet possessive caress. "Now want to argue with me about who you belong to?"

She remained completely still and concentrated on taking one breath at a time.

"But it's not really about the money, is it?" Annoyance shadowed his face and then turned into lines of implacability.

"Here's what's going to happen. You're going to finish school and come home to St. Louis, exactly as you promised. When you get there, we'll figure out what to do. But you owe me that much, Courtney, understand?"

Look for Rule's Property, coming soon.

Visit Lynda on Facebook
writelyndachance@yahoo.com
lyndachancebooks.com
Sign up for Lynda's new releases
Follow Lynda on Twitter

Other works by Lynda Chance:
Pursuit
Josh and Hannah (Redwood Falls, Book One)
And Eye for an Eye (Redwood Falls, Book Two)
The Mistress Mistake
Marco's Redemption
Sarah's Surrender
The Rancher's Virgin Acquisition
Under the Cowboy's Control
The Thrill of the Chase
Temptation in Texas: Mike and Megan
Temptation in Texas: Logan and Lauren
Staking His Claim
His Indecent Proposal
Seduced by the American Millionaire
Blackmailed Into Bed
Bedded by the Boss
The Sheriff and the Innocent Housekeeper

Printed in Great Britain
by Amazon.co.uk, Ltd.,
Marston Gate.